I0671831

Awakened

Danette Fogarty

Copywright©2015 Danette Fogarty

All Rights Reserved

ISBN# 978-0-578-16077-1

This book is dedicated to my cousin, Michelle. I'm so sorry that we couldn't find your miracle, but you showed us all how to love so completely, and never take anything for granted. Now, I realize that you were the miracle!

To Aubrey, thank you for the story.

Chapter 1

The smells, they didn't seem right. Usually her house smelled of fresh flowers. This smell was like she'd just used a whole bottle of antiseptic on something. Scrunching her nose, to show her dislike, Adalyn opened her eyes. She wanted to say something to Tommy, her fiancé about it, but no words would come out.

Her eyes only saw fog. Fear began to take over because she couldn't make out anything. Her bed usually felt so soft and comforting, but, for some reason, her back was sore and she couldn't move.

The act of opening up her eyes was enough to sap her energy, so Adalyn decided she would just go back to sleep for a little longer.

Janice saw the patient's eyes open and jumped back. "Oh my God!" She said, throwing her hands to her neck in an automatic response. When the patient's eyes closed again, and Janice was sure she was still, she left the room, running down the hall to the nurse's station. As she came to a screeching halt, the rubber on her shoes squeaking on the polished floor, she breathlessly asked, "Where's Dr. Cooper?"

Looking up calmly, Nurse Becky, wore no expression at all. Seldom, in the field of long term care, where all the patients were just basically living as vegetables, did one ever encounter an emergency. Nurse Janice's urgency annoyed her, she asked calmly, "He's in the north wing, what do you need?"

Trying to calm herself, Nurse Janice said, "The patient in Room 5 just opened her eyes and wrinkled her nose."

The information took approximately ten seconds to permeate Nurse Becky's brain. When it did, all synopses began to fire. Standing up, she pointed to Nurse Janice, "Get the EEG cart, I'll find Dr. Cooper."

Nodding, Nurse Janice ran down the hall to the room where they kept the portable equipment.

Nurse Becky picked up the phone and paged, "Dr. Cooper please call extension 36," then nervously hung up the receiver.

A few moments later, the phone rang and Becky picked it up. "This is Dr. Cooper," she heard the head of neurology announce. "Dr. Cooper, this is Becky down on the South wing, we think that the patient Phillips is showing signs of awakening."

Dr. Cooper stopped perusing the patient file he was reading, and answered, "I'll be right there," he was about to hang up when he said, "Becky, call her parents and ask them to come down here."

With a direct, "Yes, sir," Becky hung up the phone and went over to the patient files they kept nearby. It contained next of kin contacts.

Dr. Cooper arrived in Room 5 a few minutes later to find Nurse Janice hooking up the EEG electrodes to Ms. Phillips' temple. She'd already completed putting the sensors at the rear of the patient's head. "Thank you," Dr. Cooper said, glad that she seemed to understand the procedure without him having to direct her. "What did you witness?" He asked the nurse. Nurse Becky had informed him that Nurse Janice was the one who observed the patient's movement.

"I was changing out her feeding tube bag, and, when I looked down, her nose was all scrunched up," She demonstrated by distorting her face, "like when you smell something you don't like." She put the last electrode in place, and continued, "Um, then she opened her eyes, but it was like she couldn't focus. Her mouth opened as if she was about to say something, then she shut it quickly, and slipped back into her sleep state."

Intrigued, Dr. Cooper nodded. He turned on the EEG machine and watched for a few minutes.

Nurse Becky came in to say, "Her parents are on their way."

The doctor nodded, but didn't take his eyes off the machine. "Holy shit," He said loudly, then, noticing that the nurses were both looking at him, he murmured, "Sorry."

Looking over at Adalyn Phillips, he leaned down and whispered, "Okay, Adalyn, it's time to wake up." He wasn't surprised when he got no response, but he smiled anyway.

Ripping off the sheet from the machine, he instructed Nurse Janice, "Please remove the electrodes, and put the machine away." Looking at Nurse Becky, he told her, "And, please have Mr. and Mrs. Phillips come to my office as soon as they get here." He nodded when they both answered, "Yes, doctor," and went to his office to call a colleague.

Evelyn and Doug Phillips raced to the rehabilitation center as soon as they got the call. They'd had Adalyn moved there only a year ago, having wanted her to be closer to them. A lot of their friends and family put up a stink about it, saying that the smaller facility wouldn't be as helpful to Addy, but they didn't want to drive almost 5 hours every time they wanted to see her.

"Do you think this is it?" Evelyn asked her husband.

Looking over, Doug smiled at his wife of 27 years, and shook his head in denial, "No," he answered, "I think she's showing improvement."

'Funny,' Evelyn thought to herself, her husband had always been the optimist in their relationship. She'd never quite appreciated it until 3 years ago, when their family was changed forever.

Kian Fitzpatrick whistled while he came into work. A naturally upbeat person, he tried to keep his mood positive. Being a physical therapist in a place where half the patients were non-responsive, you needed to keep yourself amused. It was a great way to talk through your problems since no one talked back. Of course, he imagined that most people thought he was certifiable because he did talk to his patients as he went through their physical therapy regimen.

As he walked in the door, Kian noticed that something was different. The atmosphere was more…… "electric," was the only word he could think to describe it.

Signing in at the reception desk, Kian winked at the secretary named Molly, and went about heading down the North Wing.

His first patient, Mrs. Wilkins, was an 80 year old woman who had limited mobility due to ALS. Kian's job was to help stave off the atrophy the disease caused in Mrs. Wilkins' muscles. She was a sweet lady, but getting frustrated as the disease progressed. Even at 80, her mind was very sharp and it was very difficult for her to transition into a more sedate role, physically speaking.

"Top o'the morning to ya," Kian said, embellishing the Irish lilt in his voice.

As usual, Mrs. Wilkins giggled like a school girl, and soaked up Kian's attentions.

Looking at her physical therapist, Mrs. Wilkins said, "Kian I am ready and willing to bend to your will today."

Kian frowned, not because of Mrs. Wilkins' words, but because her tone seemed downright bright this morning. "Well, then, it's a good thing, because I was watching that show, WWE, last night and I got some good moves to bring you into submission."

Laughing at Kian's words, Mrs. Wilkins blushed. "Oh, I'll be a good girl today, I promise."

Putting his bag on the chair, Kian pulled out his folded up table, and set it up next to the bed. It was firm, with a little padding, but it helped him make sure the patients were getting the best results from the series of stretches he put them through.

He and Mrs. Wilkins went through the steps of raising her bed, so it was level with his table, and they slid her over so she was lying flat on her back. Kian grabbed a pillow from her hospital bed and gently tucked it under her head.

They started their "session" with Kian massaging her feet, then he would rotate her ankles, work on stretching her shins, and work his way up. Knees, hips, torso, hands, arms, neck, and head was last.

"You know," Mrs. Wilkins spoke while he was working on her arms, rotating them from the shoulder, "there was quite the big "to do" this morning."

Nodding, but still concentrating on his work, Kian asked, "Is that right?"

"Oh yes," Mrs. Wilkinson responded. "I guess that girl, the one in room 5 that's in the coma," she waited for Kian to nod his understanding, then she added, "Well, they said she opened her eyes."

The impact of her words, was like taking a punch to the gut for Kian. "Wha, what?" He asked in a shaky voice.

Nodding, her eyes bright with excitement, Mrs. Wilkins said, "I know, we were all just so surprised by it. They said she'd never wake up."

Finding his emotional footing, Kian tried to calm himself before asking, "Did she say anything?"

Mrs. Wilkins shook her head in denial, "No," she took a deep breath as Kian switched to her other arm, which happened to be the weakest part of her body today, then continued, "Dr. Cooper said that he's not surprised, it takes a while for the brain to "reboot," is the term I think he used."

Surprised, Kian asked her, "Did Dr. Cooper tell you all of this Mrs. Wilkins?"

Chuckling, Mrs. Wilkins answered, "Of course not, Kian, we patients eavesdrop on the nurses," she smiled, and leaned closer to whisper, "The nurses have all the good gossip."

He couldn't help it, Kian laughed. The woman was a professional at weaseling out information. He wondered, at times, if she wasn't a spy when she was younger. She would have made a very good one. "Do you think you should be talking about this then?" He asked her.

Her smile fading, Mrs. Wilkins turned to him, her face devoid of emotion, "Kian, if you sit in a rehabilitation hospital, surrounded with people who can't function, for whatever reason, for as long as I have," she pointed her finger at him, "you take whatever amusement you can get, even if that involves gossip."

Kian couldn't fault her for that. He didn't know what he would do if he wasn't able to physically move or be independent. He was pretty sure it would drive him mad quickly. "I'm sorry I doubted you," He responded in an apologetic tone.

Winking at him, Mrs. Wilkins said, "Well, maybe I'll forgive you if you massage my neck a little longer," she wiggled her eyebrows, "a woman my age doesn't get a good looking young man to massage her neck very often."

Knowing she was a sweet woman, Kian nodded and moved up to massage her neck. But, his mind was wondering about Ms. Phillips in Room 5 the whole time.

Evelyn and Doug Phillips arrived at the hospital and were met by Nurse Becky. She smiled and immediately showed them to Dr. Cooper's office. "He'll be right in," She said, and waited for them to sit down before closing the door behind her.

Dr. Cooper came in almost as soon as Nurse Becky left, a smile on his face. He greeted the Phillips with, "How are you both today?"

Evelyn cut to the quick, "Dr. Cooper, why did you ask us to come here? Is Adalyn alright?"

Sitting down at his desk, Dr. Cooper folded his hands on top of his desk, and looked at the couple for a moment before beginning to explain. "This morning, one of the nurses was changing Adalyn's medication bag when she noticed a response."

"Response?" Doug asked, leaning forward, "What kind of response?" He asked the doctor.

Evelyn grabbed her husband's hand, squeezing it.

Dr. Cooper replied, "Well, she scrunched her nose, as if she'd smelled something she didn't like," He smiled, "then she opened her eyes, and opened her mouth as if she were trying to speak."

"Oh, my Lord," Evelyn Phillips said, putting her hand over her mouth.

He could understand the Phillips' excitement. Honestly, he was just as excited and shocked as they were. But he wanted to be cautious. "Sometimes, there are stimuli that wake up the brain."

Doug asked him, "What stimuli?"

Dr. Cooper shook his head, "I don't know." He pulled out the sheet from the EEG he took this morning, and one from a month ago and placed them on the desk for Mr. and Mrs. Phillips to see. He pointed at the older one first. "Do you see how her brain waves are very consistent, with only the Theta and Delta waves detected?" He saw them nod yes, and then, answered, "That's because she's asleep and resting." Then he pointed to the scan done earlier in the day. "See this one?" He asked, "See the way there are more spikes and now her Alpha and Beta waves are showing movement." He leaned back, and said, "I've consulted with the head of Neurology at a hospital in Houston and we both agree that Adalyn, is becoming aware."

Doug and Evelyn looked at Dr. Cooper, then at each other. Then they started laughing and hugged one another.

"Now don't get too excited yet," Dr. Cooper warned, "She may never be fully awake, but from what I've read, the odds have certainly improved."

Nodding, Evelyn asked, "Can we see her?"

Dr. Cooper stood up, and smiled, "Of course," he held out his hand to lead the way, "Let's go."

They went down the hall quickly, and entered Adalyn's room. It was bright in here, as insisted on by her mother, Evelyn. Addy always liked bright colors and natural light so Evelyn came in about a month after her daughter was admitted, and painted the room. An artist friend of Addy's offered to do a mural of a field of flowers as well, so one of the walls looked like it was a spring meadow.

Evelyn went over to the bed, and sat down. She took Addy's hand into her own and said, "Baby, it's Momma."

When there was no response, Evelyn looked up at Dr. Cooper. "This is why I was telling you not to get too excited, it could be a long, slow process for her."

Looking at his wife, Doug smiled. This was the first good news they'd received in the three years since Adalyn's car accident. This whole ordeal had been hell on their family and he knew both Addy and his wife deserved better. "We'll try to keep it calm," He said to Dr. Cooper, then stepped up behind his wife to rub her shoulders.

Chapter 2

The smell was back and Adalyn opened her eyes once again. She wanted her fiancé to put in some air freshener or something, anything to get rid of the pungent odor. It was like an unclean bathroom or something. Picking up her hand, she tried to rub her nose, but her hand was so heavy that she could only move it a little bit.

She opened her eyes again, and it was bright. Not like looking into the sun, bright, but like looking into a sunny pasture after a rainy day, kind of bright. There were flowers, she could see them now. But if there were flowers, why did it smell so bad?

Exhausted, Adalyn decided to just go back to sleep. It would be better in the morning, she was sure of it.

Kian did his usual rounds and waited to go into Room 5 until last. Adalyn's parents were in there, visiting, and he didn't want to interrupt their time with their daughter.

He worked with a lot of patients that were impeded physically, but they were still communicative. To work with a patient, like Adalyn Phillips, was a different experience altogether.

First, he had to know what her limits were physically, because she wasn't able to tell him if something hurt. She'd been in a coma for two years before coming here and he'd been her primary physical therapist for the last year. Just seeing her evoked feelings in him he wasn't sure he was able to confront, but he did it. Certainly, the fact that she didn't talk back, or even know he was there, helped.

After going into the room, he pulled out the bottle of lotion Adalyn's mother asked him to use. It was her favorite scent, Mrs. Phillips told Kian; plumeria. Adalyn had gone to Hawaii for her job and had fallen in love with the scent, so Mrs. Phillips asked that he use it. And now, every time he smelled plumeria, he thought of Adalyn Phillips.

"Good afternoon," He greeted Adalyn, when he entered the room. "I've been told," He started to explain, "that you gave the staff quite a little flutter earlier today," he pulled the sheet down so he could work on her feet first.

Massaging her muscles loosened them up for the exercises. The nurses would turn the patients on a regular timed rotation to prevent bed sores or muscle issues, but it wasn't like what he did. He stretched every muscle group there was and kept the muscles in good working order in case the patient needed to use them again.

Within minutes the smell from the lotion permeated the room. Kian was still at the foot of the bed, chatting about what Mrs. Wilkins told him. When he happened to glance up, Adalyn's eyes were open.

The smell was heavenly and Adalyn preferred it to the other smells she'd had recently. When she was able to open her eyes, she saw a man sitting at the end of her bed. Why was he in her room? Her eyes focused past him and saw the flowers, so she wondered why they were outside. He was rubbing her feet, and it felt so good.

He stood up and moved closer to her face. He was saying something because she could see his lips moving, but she couldn't make it out. 'What was that?' She asked him, but realized her lips wouldn't work.

Kian stood up and went up to the head of the bed, "Mo Milis," he crooned. It was an endearment his mother used when he was a child, it meant, 'my love.' She didn't answer, but she stared at him very intensely. She had blue eyes, he noticed. Since she'd never been awake before, he never knew how spectacular the color of her eyes were. He'd seen pictures of her from before the accident, but it was not like seeing into the real thing. Then her eyes drifted shut and Kian stood there, just staring.

For the rest of his session with Adalyn, Kian kept looking at her face, hoping she would awaken again. But, she didn't. He went through the exercises, as prescribed by his boss, Dr. Tillman, and then went to find the doctor to explain what happened.

"Dr. Cooper?" Kian asked him as he rounded the corner.

Surprised, Dr. Cooper stopped mid-stride, and looked up. "Oh, Kian, how are you today?" He asked.

"Fine," Kian answered, "I was just working with Ms. Phillips in Room 5," he started.

Dr. Cooper smiled, "Oh, so you heard about her "development" this morning," he said, then added, "from Mrs. Wilkins, no doubt."

Nodding, Kian answered, "Yes, but I wanted to let you know, she opened her eyes when I was in there doing her exercises."

As if he was just splashed with cold water, Dr. Cooper's demeanor changed. "Why didn't you notify one of the staff?" He demanded of Kian as he started rushing down the hall toward Adalyn's room.

Following Dr. Cooper, Kian felt stupid for not acting sooner. They rushed into the room and Dr. Cooper checked Adalyn's vitals while Kian just stood there and watched.

"Tell me exactly what happened?" Dr. Cooper asked him.

Walking around to the end of the bed, Kian explained that he was massaging Adalyn's feet with the lotion her mother requested he use, when her eyes opened. He spoke to her and her mouth moved, but no words came out.

Nodding, Dr. Cooper grabbed her chart and made some notes, asking Kian, "What time did this occur?"

Kian told the doctor everything he could. Afterwards, he grabbed his bag, along with his table, and left the center.

On the drive home, Kian wondered what Adalyn was thinking when he was talking to her. Clearly, she was confused, but she was there, and definitely aware. For that, he was grateful.

The next day, Nurse Suzie was on duty. She'd gone over all her patients' info with Nurse Becky and was making the rounds and everything seemed pretty quiet.

Apparently Mr. and Mrs. Phillips were on their way to the center, to see their daughter, Adalyn, in Room 5, but they weren't expected for a while yet.

After checking the medication charts, Suzie had to go into Adalyn's room to change her IV bag. It was a sunny day, so Suzie decided she'd open up the blinds to let in the beautiful sunlight. As she turned around, she saw that Adalyn's eyes were open, and she was staring right at Suzie. So shocked, by the patient's actions, Suzie yelped.

Rushing over to the bed, she tried to calm herself, and smile down at Adalyn. She took the young woman's hand and rubbed it calmly, saying, "Hello, Adalyn, you're safe here." She didn't see a change in Adalyn's expression, but she added, "I'm Suzie."

Adalyn smiled, then closed her eyes again.

Noting the time, Suzie rushed out to the nursing station and told the charge nurse, Pam, what happened. They called Dr. Cooper, to tell him of the development.

An hour later, Evelyn and Doug Phillips showed up to the rehabilitation center to see their daughter. Evelyn brought in some clothes and belongings that were in Adalyn's apartment before the accident, but now, were stored at their house. Doug didn't want to get his hopes up, so he indulged his wife's plans, but didn't encourage her.

"Oh, Mr. and Mrs. Phillips," Suzie said as she came into the room. She smiled at Adalyn's parents. "She opened her eyes again today," She said, "and about scared the wits right out of me."

Doug spoke first, "What?" He asked the nurse.

Walking over to take Adalyn's pulse, Suzie explained, "I was opening up the blinds because it's such a beautiful day out, and, when I turned around, she was staring at me."

Evelyn started crying, and asked, "Really?"
Suzie nodded, "Yes, then I walked over and told her she was safe and that my name was Suzie." She winked at Mrs.

Phillips, and continued, "And she smiled at me, then closed her eyes again."

Tears streaming down her face, Evelyn held her daughter's hand, "Oh Lord," she whispered, "bring our girl back to us."

Doug said his own silent prayers and sat on the other side of his daughter's bed, thoughts racing around in his head.

Suzie left the room so Adalyn's parents could be alone with their daughter. She wished, for their sakes, that Adalyn would wake up. The odds weren't in their favor, but miracles did happen.

Adalyn heard her mom's voice and opened her eyes. She'd missed her mom, even though they saw each other once a week, she'd been so busy lately, that she'd not been able to see her. It was fuzzy, but her mom leaned closer, and Adalyn could see her clearly.

"Doug!" Evelyn shouted, rousing her husband from his nap.

He hadn't even realized he dozed off, so, being startled, Doug jumped up, asking "What?"

Without leaving her daughter, Evelyn motioned for her husband to come over. As he rounded the bed, it was clear that Adalyn's eyes were open. "Sweet Jesus," Doug said.

'Daddy,' Adalyn thought to herself. 'You're here.' She loved being around her dad. He was funny and always softened her mother's tense edges. She wanted to stay awake and talk to them, but she was so tired. It was so good to see them. Her eyes drifted closed, and she willed them to open. Her lips moving, she wanted to say, "Mommy," but it came out as a gurgle.

Doug Phillips ran out into the hall, and yelled at the nurse, "Get a doctor in here, she opened her eyes and tried to talk."

Nurse Suzie dialed the physician on call, who came down to the room within minutes. His name was Dr. Peters, and he was doing a medical rotation here on the days when Dr. Cooper was off.

Dr. Peters came into the room, spoke to Adalyn's parents, and asked them what happened. He'd love to be as excited as they were about what was going on with their daughter, but he was skeptical by nature, and with this kind of brain injury, he didn't hold out much hope.

As soon as the doctor left the room, Evelyn turned to her husband, and said, "He doesn't believe she'll come out of this."

Doug agreed with his wife, but he'd seen his little girl's eyes open and knew she recognized him, so he didn't give a flying flip what the doctor thought. "I know, but we need to believe."

Evelyn nodded, and kissed her daughter's hand. "Baby, it's Mom. If you want to wake up, we'll help you. You've been sleeping so long, sweet girl, and we miss you."

Hearing the agony in his wife's voice, Doug had to fight back his own tears. The doctor may be skeptical, but they weren't. "We'll get some stuff together from the house, and stay up here starting tomorrow," He told Evelyn.

"Thank you," She whispered to her husband.

They sat with Adalyn for hours, hoping that she'd open her eyes one more time, but she didn't.

On the third day, Dr. Cooper came in and started a series of tests to be done on Adalyn. If she was, in fact, coming out of the coma, then she should respond to stimuli.

He did the standard tests of rubbing his knuckles on her sternum, and she twitched. A good sign. Next, he used a pen and ran it up the bottom of her foot. There was some reflexive response, and he was stunned. None of his colleagues ever had a patient come out of a coma after 3 years. It was new territory, at least in the medical circles he was involved in, and he wanted to make sure he gave Adalyn the very best chance at recovery.

After getting the nurses to order some blood tests, he called her parents and set up a meeting.

Evelyn and Doug were supportive of whatever could be done to assist their daughter.

Kian came into work, and the place was abuzz with the talk of the "coma girl waking up."

His own response to the news was mixed. He'd been working with Adalyn Phillips for a year now. He had no fear that her muscles would respond well to treatment, it was her mind that he worried about. Traumatic brain injury was a tricky thing; he'd worked with vets who suffered from it, and it could go either way.

Deciding to start the day in the South Wing, which meant he'd be in Adalyn's room early, he greeted the nursing staff, and went into his first patient's room.

It was mid-morning when he got to Adalyn's room. Her parents were not here yet, or had stepped out. The nurses said they were staying in the area now that she'd started responding.

He was unpacking his bag, putting the lotion on the table beside the bed, when Dr. Cooper came in.

"Good morning, Kian," Dr. Cooper said, then asked, "Any response from our patient yet?"

Shaking his head no, Kian responded, "Not yet, but I haven't done much either."

Dr. Cooper nodded, and smiled. "Do you mind if I observe you today?" He asked Kian.

"No, not at all," Was Kian's response, but he didn't like having people watch him.

Sometimes it was family members who believed he was "hurting" their loved one, or sometimes he'd had doctors ask him, "What's the point?" So now, he was naturally reluctant to open himself up to possible criticism.

Starting with Adalyn's feet, Kian applied the lotion and started massaging them. For him, it was just part of his job, so his mind wandered as he did it. He was wondering what it would be like if Adalyn did wake up? Could he tell her everything he needed to say? Lord knew he'd done it while she was asleep. Can someone remember what you say to them if they're in a coma?

Rotating Adalyn's ankles, Kian started the exercises. He lifts her legs, one at a time, and had her do knee lifts and extended her feet to stretch out her Achilles tendon.

"So," Dr. Cooper asked, "What got you into physical therapy?"

Coming out of his "working trance," Kian smiled, and answered, "My parents. They both needed physical therapy and it seemed easier to get the schooling and do it myself."

Nodding, Dr. Cooper commented, "I've never heard that reason before, nice one."

Kian always liked Dr. Cooper. He was a straightforward person who didn't criticize or demean people. Working around doctors all the time, Kian had seen the gamut. The ego-maniacs down to the passive, but Dr. Cooper was, by far, one of the best. Looking over at him, Kian asked, "Do you think she'll come out of this?"

Dr. Cooper sighed, and said, "I'm not 100% sure, but she looks good."

Nodding, Kian put down Adalyn's leg, and started in on her right hand. He was rubbing the palm, when he felt her fingers close around his hand. Silently, he looked over at Dr. Cooper, who was motioning for him to keep rubbing her hand.

Adalyn's hand tingled. It felt so good. And she heard that lyrical voice again. There was another voice too, one she didn't recognize. She wanted to hold the hand that was making hers feel so good so she willed her fingers to close. When she did, the rubbing continued. Something flickered inside of her, something she couldn't recognize. Then, the voice was asking her something. "Open your eyes Adalyn," It was saying. She wanted to so badly to open them, but they wouldn't cooperate.

Chapter 3

The next couple of days were quiet. Adalyn didn't move, didn't open her eyes, and showed no signs of response. The staff's mood seemed to sink with each day of quiet.

Kian came in one of the days and did his exercises with Adalyn. He half expected her to squeeze his hand again or open her eyes, but there was nothing. He talked to her, telling her that she needed to rest, and everyone would just need to understand it took a little bit to wake up after 3 years.

As he was leaving, he ran into Mrs. Phillips.

"Oh, Kian," Evelyn said, using his given name as he asked her too last year. She asked him, "How are you today?"

Nodding hello, Kian replied, "I'm fit as a fiddle, Mrs. Phillips, and how are you this fine day?"

Evelyn always thought Kian was devilishly handsome, and so exciting with his Irish accent. He had a reddish hue to his hair, which probably endured her to him because Addy had red hair as well. "Any news on our girl today?" She asked Kian, hope lacing her words.

Sighing, Kian answered, "I'm afraid not, ma'am." He winked at her, and added, "But I'm not one to give up easily, and it seems to me that you and Mr. Phillips aren't either. If Ms. Adalyn got any of that from you, she'll be just fine."

Maybe it was his accent, or just his positive attitude, but Evelyn felt that if Kian could be assured of Adalyn's recovery, then she had no business doubting it. She smiled at him, and said, "You have a point, Kian."

Kian allowed her to pass, and hoped, for her parents' sake, that Adalyn did wake up.

Since the center was his last stop for the day, Kian went home.

His apartment was just a few blocks from downtown, Pearland, Texas. It was close enough for him to commute to most of the main medical facilities around Houston, but far enough from the rush of living in a huge city.

As he parked his car, Kian got out, and turned to walk over to the mail boxes. He got his mail, and ran into his neighbor, Missy. "Good afternoon," He said pleasantly.

Missy blushed. She'd been living in the same apartment complex as Kian for over two years now, and she was completely in love with him. Of course, she was too shy to say anything; she'd really only observed him from afar. "Hi, Kian,' she replied, in a shy tone.

Kian always thought that his neighbor was a sweet lady, even if she didn't say much and seemed flustered every time she was around him. "Well," He waved, "You have a beautiful rest of your day."

Nodding, Missy waved back, but didn't say anything.

By the time Kian got upstairs, into his apartment, he was tired and ready to relax.

After turning on the television, to provide some background noise, Kian turned on his computer, and then went into the kitchen. Dinner was usually easy, something that could be cooked in the microwave, ordered in, or a donation from Missy. Tonight he decided on some leftover stew he'd actually made a few days earlier. It was Irish stew, from his mother's recipe. Lately, he'd been thinking about his parents a lot, and the stew made him feel like they were still there.

It was Adalyn Phillips that prompted the memories, he was sure of it. If she woke up, then things would change. He shouldn't care, but he did.

Sitting at the table, and eating his stew, Kian thought that he'd better figure out, what he would say to her, and soon.

Adalyn wanted to wake up. She tried, hearing voices, and noises around her, but she was so tired. Finally, she felt like she was strong enough to get up. She opened her eyes. It was pretty dark in the room, a dim light was somewhere behind her and barely illuminated her surroundings. She could see she was in a bed, but it looked like a hospital bed. Why would she be in a hospital bed? Feeling stiff, she looked around the room, trying to get her eyes to focus. There was a chair in the corner, a television hung up on a wall across from her. It was hard to see, but it looked like the wall opposite her was painted with flowers. Is that what she saw the other day? Was it even the other day? How long had she been here?

She moved her arms, although it felt strange to move them, she found her muscles weren't as stiff as she thought they felt. Maybe it was because of the rubbing she felt. Was that today, or much earlier? Her mind was foggy, not being able to focus on events.

Reaching up, Adalyn touched her face, and her head. She had a dull ache at the back of it. She was about to sit up, when she heard a noise coming from her right side. Looking over, she saw a woman enter the room.

Nurse Janice walked into Ms. Phillips' room, just to check on her. She almost dropped the bag she held in her hands when she saw Adalyn Phillips staring at her. "Well, you're up," She said, trying to sound calm so she didn't startle Adalyn.

Adalyn nodded, and said, "Y....es." Her voice sounded strange to her, and her throat was dry.

The shock on Janice's face must have registered with Adalyn because she started to shake. Rushing over to the bed, Janice sat down beside Adalyn and took her hands. She rubbed them, partially to put the young woman at ease, and partially to put herself at ease. "A lot of people have been waiting for you to wake up," Janice told her.

Adalyn smiled, and asked the woman, "Who?" She wanted to ask, 'Who are you?' but the words wouldn't come.

Seeing the young woman's agitation, Janice helped her get comfortable by getting up and retrieving another pillow from the cabinet, and putting it behind her head. "You just rest now," She said, "I'm going to be back in just a little bit," Janice told her.

As soon as Adalyn's head was repositioned, she drifted back off to sleep. Janice ran out of the room, and down to the nurse's station.

Later, that day, Evelyn and Doug came into the center to a flurry of "hellos" and big smiles.

Dr. Cooper met them at the nurse's station outside of Adalyn's room. "We've got some good news," He told them.

Evelyn's eyes flew to her daughter's room, excitement rippling through her chest. Doug's arm was wrapped around her shoulders; as if to protect her.

Janice came around the counter of the nurse's station, and said, "Mr. and Mrs. Phillips, I spoke to her this morning."

"Spoke?" Doug asked immediately.

Nodding, and wearing a huge smile, Janice added, "I came in this morning to check her vitals, and she was sort of leaning forward, and she said "yes," and asked "who," but I think she was trying to ask who I was."

Shock washed over Evelyn. She didn't listen to anymore; she turned and went directly into her daughter's room. "Addy," She pleaded, as she sat down on her daughter's bed, "Please wake up, baby."

Doug stood at the doorway, looking into the room, tears flowing down his cheeks. When Addy was like this, so still, and no signs of understanding, it was hard to have faith. He wanted to be like Evelyn, just believing that she would wake up and things will go back to how they were before the terrible accident.

Dr. Cooper came up behind Mr. Phillips and placed a hand on his shoulder. "It's looking very positive," He told him.

Doug looked over at Addy's doctor, and took a deep breath. "Let's hope so," He said, "for all of our sakes."

Evelyn sat there, next to her daughter, and waited. When her husband asked her to go with him to get some lunch, she politely declined. She watched the nurses come in and out periodically, checking Addy's vitals. They would smile at her, and Evelyn knew they felt pity for her. She just didn't care, she only wanted her daughter back, and, if there was even the slightest chance of that happening, she'd sit here until she was eighty.

Darkness was starting to envelope the outside, when Evelyn stood up to shut the blinds. She stood there, looking out the window, watching the fading light drop down over the horizon, and wondered how Addy would feel, when she did come fully awake. She was about to turn and pick up a magazine when she heard a noise. Turning back around, Evelyn watched as her daughter, who had been sleeping for 3 long years, was now facing her.

"Ma…..ma," Adalyn said in a small voice.

Hearing her daughter's voice, after all that time, was overwhelming. Her hand over her mouth, Evelyn began to sob. "Oh, baby," She said through her tears, "I'm here." Walking over, she sat down next to Addy.

Emotional, for some reason she couldn't explain, Adalyn started to cry. It felt strange, as if she hadn't done it in a long time. But, the reality of her mom sitting next to her, holding her, soothed her uncertainty.

Doug Phillips came back from getting some food, and walked into his daughter's room. The vision of his wife, holding their daughter, shook him to his core. He dropped the bag, with the food in it.

The noise made Addy jump. She turned her head, slowly, and her eyes met those of her father. She smiled, and said, "Da, a, ad."

Crying, because, although her voice was rough, and it was obviously an effort, his little girl just said, Dad.

Crossing over to the bed, Doug took his little girl into his arms, "Hello there, toots," He whispered his nickname for Addy into her ear, and cried like a child.

Pam, the nurse on duty, walked into Ms. Phillips' room and wanted to jump for joy at the sight of Adalyn's parents holding her. It was clear that she was awake. Backing out of the room, slowly, Pam went out to the nurse's station, and called Dr. Cooper.

Within minutes Adalyn was exhausted. She didn't understand why she couldn't move the way she wanted to, or why she was so tired. She just knew that she needed to go back to sleep.

Her parents helped her settle down into her bed. As sleep overtook her, Addy remembered hearing another voice, but just couldn't muster the energy to stay awake.

Evelyn and Doug stood outside their daughter's room and spoke to Dr. Cooper. With Evelyn's excitement evident, she asked, "What now?"

Shrugging, and feeling silly for not knowing exactly what to tell Mr. and Mrs. Phillips, Dr. Cooper answered, "I'm not sure."

He nodded toward Adalyn's room, "It could be days, weeks, or months, or…." He hesitated.

"Or?" Doug asked.

Sighing, Dr. Cooper answered, "Or this could be a fluke and she goes back to her previous sleep state." He put his hand on Mrs. Phillips' shoulder, and smiled. "Honestly, I've got calls into a few neurologists who've had patients come to after long bouts of coma states, but it's still a mystery as to how the mind heals itself."

Frustrated, Doug retorted, "So, basically, you're covering your butt in case she really doesn't improve."

"Believe me," Dr. Cooper said, a little sharply, "I want her to wake up as much as you do." He tried to calm down. "I'm just saying there isn't a whole lot of precedence for this and I don't want any of us to get our hopes up."

Evelyn looked at her husband, smiled, then looked directly at Dr. Cooper, and replied, "I think it's a little late for that now." She wasn't going to be told there was no hope now, not after this. Without waiting for any response, she left the men in the hallway, and went back into her daughter's room.

Kian came in the next morning, not in the best of moods. Normally he was a light-hearted person who believed in decency and being polite, but this morning's events tested even his limits.

The lady at the coffee shop was rude, he was almost rear ended by some woman who insisted on doing her makeup while driving, and his tire was almost flat.

Without his usual greeting to the administrative staff, he quietly signed in and headed straight for room 5.

Chapter 4

"Oh, Kian," Mrs. Phillips said as he entered the room.

Surprised by the presence of Adalyn's mother this early, Kian grimaced inwardly. He didn't really relish the thought of having an audience this morning until he was able to shake this bad mood. Trying to be polite, Kian responded, "Good morning, Mrs. Phillips."

Smiling, Evelyn asked, "Rough morning?"

Kian was surprised by her quick assessment of his mood. "Yes," He answered.

Sitting back down beside her daughter's bed, Evelyn sighed. "Yeah, me too," She offered.

He set down his bag and his table and walked over to the bathroom to wash his hands. After he came out, he asked Mrs. Phillips, "Would you like to talk about it?"

Evelyn looked up from watching her daughter, and stared at Kian intently. "I'm pretty sure it's not a big stretch as to what I'm stressing over," She nodded toward Adalyn. "She sat up and hugged me, talked to me, and yet Dr. Cooper thinks we shouldn't get our hopes up."

Sitting down at the end of the bed, Kian rubbed his hands together to warm them, before he reached in his bag for the plumeria lotion. "May I ask," Kian started, then began rubbing Adalyn's feet, "what exactly they would like you to do?"

Smiling, for the first time, since she spoke to her daughter, Evelyn nodded. "I don't know." And she laughed.

"Mama," Adalyn spoke, causing both Evelyn and Kian to look over at her.

Leaning forward, Evelyn smiled, "Hello, sweet girl."

Kian couldn't move, couldn't speak, he could only watch the interaction and witness the love between mother and daughter; and it broke his heart.

Getting up quietly, Kian left the room, in order to get Dr. Cooper.

Ten minutes later, Kian was still standing outside of Adalyn's room, when Dr. Cooper came out. He looked at Kian, and smiled. "Well, it seems our miracle patient is awake," He shook his head, as he walked toward the nurse's station, as if he still couldn't believe it.

Mr. Phillips showed up, nodded his greeting to Kian, and then went into the room.

Kian didn't want to disturb them, but he needed to get his bag and table so he could visit his other patients.

Quietly, so as not to disturb them, Kian went into the room. He stopped almost immediately, shocked at what he was seeing. There, sat Adalyn, only this time she was leaning forward. As she turned, to look at Kian, her hair fell down over her shoulders. The blinds on the window were open, shedding light behind her, and Kian thought she looked like one of those mystical mermaids from tales his mother told him as a child. He smiled, and moved forward.

Adalyn saw the man come into the room. He was tall, and had a strong face. She remembered that he was the one with the accent and tried to smile.

"Ms. Phillips," Kian said brightly, "I think your parents have been waiting for you to wake up."

The sound of his voice, so quick and musical, made Adalyn giggle. Hearing herself make the noise almost startled her.

Mr. Phillips came over to Kian and clapped him on the shoulder. He whispered, "The doctor thinks she's finally awakened."

The feelings that ran through Kian filled him completely. She'd been like this dream he could witness a couple of days a week, talking to her, and watching her, and feeling safe about it. Now that she was awake, there was something inside of him that he couldn't tuck away, as he normally would.

Evelyn smiled, and spoke to her daughter, "Addy, this is Kian."

Adalyn turned the man's name over in her mind a few times. She wasn't sure she could pronounce it, but she tried,

"Kee," she got out, and was frustrated because she couldn't form the rest of his name.

Smiling, Kian stepped forward, "I'm sorry to interrupt you, I'm just needing to get my things, and I'll be on my way."

Evelyn nodded; her smile wide. "Of course, I'm sorry," She looked at Kian, "we must have messed up your schedule."

Looking over at Mrs. Phillips, Kian answered, "Oh, I think I'll let it go this time." He winked at Adalyn, "This is kind of a big event."

Doug chuckled and brought in a glass of ice water for Addy. He handed it to her, and glanced over at Kian, to say, "Kind of a big thing."

Grabbing his things, Kian smiled to the family one more time before heading out. His mood had certainly improved. Sometimes it just took seeing a miracle to make you realize how Blessed you really were.

Adalyn sat with her parents for the rest of the day. Every time she started to feel tired, she moved, or drank water, or tried to eat a little something; anything to keep from going back to sleep. It was like she was desperate to stay awake.

She wasn't able to form full words, so trying to communicate with her mom and dad was frustrating her. She could mumble simple words like, mama and dad, and other one syllable words like who, like, and yum. Her parents were patient, but they didn't say much, and didn't answer the questions that kept running through her mind. She wanted to know how long she'd been asleep, she wondered where Tommy, her fiancé, was, and she wanted to ask why she felt so strange. The doctor came in, although she couldn't remember his name, and he explained that it would take a while for her to feel "normal" again.

As the sun slipped away, settling down for the night, Adalyn couldn't fight the pull of sleep. She hoped that she would wake up again; there was a fear deep inside of her that made her think she may not. Her parents sat on either side of her as she drifted off, smiling at her, just like when she was a little girl. It was hard to leave them, even for the necessity of sleep.

Kian finished his day, but he couldn't really recall much about it. He accomplished his tasks, even met with his supervisor to go over some patients' records, but his mind was definitely elsewhere. It was in a room, watching an angelic woman look at him for the first time.

He sat on the sofa, in his apartment, and tried to think of what she must be going through, all the confusion and questions she must have. Before drifting off to sleep himself, the drone of the television lulling him into a semi-conscious state, Kian wondered what she would think if she knew everything.

Adalyn woke up, and saw a pretty woman standing near her bed, holding her wrist. "Good morning," The woman said, in a bright voice that prompted Adalyn to smile. She tried to respond, but it sounded like, "Goo monin."

"That was really good," Nurse Janice responded. She was amazed that, after three years of being unconscious, Ms. Phillips had the ability to understand and make any sense. "You just take your time," She assured Adalyn, "you'll get the hang of it soon enough." With a wink, she made some notes on the laptop near the bed, and left the room.

Looking around the room, Addy knew her mother must have helped decorate it. The bright colors and that wall of flowers were amazing; just looking around the room made Addy feel happy. The blinds were still drawn shut, but Adalyn could make out rays of sunlight edging the window, and she yearned to get up and walk outside.

Checking the doorway, and not seeing anyone in the nearby vicinity, Addy started to wonder if she could do it; get up and make her way to the window. It only seemed to be about 6 feet away, so it was really only about ten steps or so, right?

Moving her arms first, Addy managed to get the covers pulled down. It took a bit to get her mind and body to sync up again. Focusing, she slowly moved her legs to the right. Her thought was, if she could get her legs to the edge of the bed, gravity should help her along.

She was breaking a sweat, a few minutes later, and had only been able to move her legs halfway to the edge of the bed. Mad, because her body didn't want to move, tears started down her cheeks.

Kian knew he would see Adalyn Phillips first today. After meeting with his supervisor, and basically missing her session yesterday, they needed to step up her revised physical therapy regimen. It wasn't a matter of staving off muscle atrophy; now it was a fight to get Ms. Phillips' muscles to start working fully again so she could actually use them.

As Kian entered the room, he saw her leaning forward, and trying to move her legs off the bed with her arms. She was crying and panic filled Kian's chest, making him jump into action. "Ms. Phillips," He called, making her jump. "Ya don't need to be gettin up so quickly, now." Moving over to her side, he slid her legs back up onto the bed, a safe distance from the edge.

Since Addy wasn't able to form words fully, she pointed to the window, and mumbled, "Ssss, su, su," and was getting even madder at her lack of ability in speaking.

Looking behind him, Kian tried to figure out what she was saying. He smiled, and turned back toward her, and asked, "Do ya want to see the sunlight?"

Relieved that he got her meaning, Addy nodded eagerly.

With a smile pasted on his face, Kian crossed over to the window and opened up the blinds. Bright, warm sunlight poured into the room. And, once again, he saw Adalyn Phillips, surrounded with sunlight, and yet, even the sunlight, created by the Almighty, seemed to pale in comparison to her.

He walked back over to the bed, trying to look stern, and said, "Now, ya can't be up and around by yerself just yet."

Adalyn nodded dutifully, but they both knew she wasn't going to listen.

Seeing the defiance in her eyes only made her more attractive, in Kian's mind. "Plus," He added, looking at the wires hooked up to her body, "Ya still have in your catheter and yer all hooked up there," he pointed to the heart monitor and blood pressure machine.

Understanding what the word catheter meant, Adalyn blushed. "So.....sor," She grunted.

"It's just fine," Kian said soothingly, and tucked the blanket around her. "If it's the outside you wish to see, we'll put in a request with Dr. Cooper and maybe we can do some of our exercises out there." He wanted to give her a minute to compose herself, so he walked out of the room, and headed to the nurse's station.

Addy sat in her bed, feeling foolish. She needed to slow down, and do whatever it took to get better. Understanding the words was okay, but using them in her speech was very difficult.

She appreciated that the man with the beautiful speech seemed to understand her. He was so tall, under different circumstances, she might even be fearful of his size, but there was something kind in his eyes and in the way he moved that reassured her.

Kian spoke to the nurses, and passed on Adalyn's request to go outside. Nurse Janice smiled her apology, but said they couldn't let Adalyn go outside until the doctor's placed the order for her to be taken off her machines.

With a look of irritation, he nodded and returned to Adalyn's room. He tried to put a smile on his face, but it was a façade since he knew he couldn't give her what she wanted. "I'm sorry, mo mhuirnin," He walked over to the side of Addy's bed, "we'll have to be waiting until Dr. Cooper gives us the go ahead for you to go outside."

Even though Addy didn't understand whatever language he was speaking, she felt as though it was meant to soothe her. She nodded in understanding.

"Not the patient type, are ye?" Kian asked her as he set up his table, trying to find something to keep him busy so he didn't stare at her.

His comment touched Adalyn's funny bone, and she made a half giggle sound, while shaking her head no.

After setting up his table, Kian stood next to the bed and replied, "That's what my mind was thinking." He clapped his hands together, "Now," he started, "we are going to be doing a lot of exercises since you're awake." He handed her a sheet of paper that had pictures of different body positions, "This should help you get an idea of what we'll be after." As he stood there, watching Adalyn stare at the paper, he asked her, "Can you understand what yer lookin at there?"

Adalyn could focus, and it took a minute or so for her to recognize the different body parts; arm, leg, hand, foot. She finally nodded. "Ye.....sss," She managed.

Smiling again, Kian answered, "That's good Ms. Phillips, real good." Helping her shift from the hospital bed onto his table, Kian began by rotating her feet.

As he moved through the series of exercises, it occurred to him, that Adalyn was watching him intently. "I know speakin isn't coming easy to you just now," He rubbed her foot to loosen up the muscles, "but you'll have it soon enough."

Watching this man, as he got her body to move in ways that she wasn't able to made Addy mad but also made her curious. Curious about him and why he was here. He was very handsome, she thought, then got upset with herself for thinking such a thing when she was engaged to Tommy.

Noticing a change in Adalyn's facial expression, Kian asked, "Am I hurting you?" When she shook her head no, he continued, but it was clear that she was upset by something. "If ye have any questions about anything, I'm here to answer them."

Staring at this stranger, Adalyn wondered if she'd ever be able to ask the questions she needed the answers to. For the rest of her session, she simply stared off into space, wondering, about everything.

Chapter 5

That evening Kian received an email from his supervisor, requesting his attendance at a meeting the next morning. All of the medical staff directly associated with Ms. Phillips was having a meeting to discuss her care.

After his morning session with Adalyn, and feeling low about not getting her outside, as she'd requested, his mind was all amuck for the rest of the day. He did his job, did it quite well, but his mind was miles away, thinking of the beautiful redhead who looked so helpless.

The next morning, Kian met his supervisor, Dr. Tillman, before going into the conference room at the rehabilitation center. They were joined by several doctors who nodded, then took a seat. As soon as Dr. Cooper entered, with another doctor, from the looks of him, they started. Dr. Cooper spoke first.

"I think we're all surprised at the amazing recovery of Ms. Phillips, and, as we've never had this type of recovery before here, I'd like to tread carefully with her rehabilitation, at least for now." He took a breath, and was about to say something else, when he saw Kian's hand raised, "Yes, Kian?" He asked.

Nodding to Dr. Cooper, out of respect, Kian asked, "Since it's Ms. Phillips we're all here discussing, shouldn't she be here so she can understand the goals of this group?"

"I hardly think," Another one of the doctors started, before he was given a harsh look by Dr. Cooper. After looking back at Kian, Dr. Cooper replied, "Kian, I think that's an excellent idea."

Within minutes the group of them were going down the hall toward Adalyn's room. Her parents were in the room with her, and they all three looked surprised when the group of doctors, along with Kian and another therapist, entered the room.

Dr. Cooper smiled, and said, "Ms. Phillips, we were just discussing a rehabilitation schedule for you, and Kian here, suggested that we include you in on the meeting." He watched as Adalyn nodded, "It's clear you understand, so we'll begin. "First," he pointed to the doctor to his right, "This is Dr. Gruen, and she's responsible for getting your speech back."

"Ms. Phillips," Dr. Gruen stepped forward and shook Adalyn's hand, "we think you have what's called Broca's Aphasia, meaning that the part of your brain that was damaged has to do with your speech function but you're still able to read and understand the language that you hear." She waited for Adalyn to nod, then continued with, "So, we're going to have our speech therapist, Ms. Westin, come in every day and work with you." Squeezing Adalyn's hand in comfort, she added, "We don't know if you'll get all of your speech back, but we're hopeful."

Evelyn's hand flew to her chest, in a feeble attempt to fight back her emotions. She could see that Addy knew what was wrong with her, but to be trapped inside her mind must be agony.

Dr. Cooper pointed to Dr. Tillman, "This is Dr. Tillman, he and Kian," gesturing to include Kian, "are going to put you through some paces over the next couple of days, to see what you can do, and what we need to help your body remember to do." He winked at Adalyn, "But, I can tell you, young lady, from what we've seen you do so far, we're all pretty impressed."

Listening to each one of the doctors talk to her, Addy felt a little overwhelmed, but also relieved that she was being told why she couldn't do certain things. After her parents explained that she'd been in a coma for three years, she'd sat there, quietly, for a long time. Three years? How could it have been three years when, for her, it felt like only a couple of days ago?

The last thing she could clearly remember was being at the bridal shop with her mother, her best friend, Jeni, and her cousin, Michelle, for her final wedding dress fitting. Michelle was going to be her maid of honor, while Jeni was her bridesmaid. They were all giddy with excitement over the dresses.

Then, there was nothing, as if there was a huge hole in her head the size of the Grand Canyon. It scared her, feeling all that blackness fill her mind. She looked at her parents, at all the doctors standing around her, and gave them a thumbs up.

The room erupted into laughter.

After the meeting with Adalyn, her parents, and the doctors, Kian went back to Dr. Tillman's office so they could hash out the tests for Adalyn. Dr. Cooper was going to have her removed from the feeding tube, the catheter, and any other machine that might impede her movement.

She would need a few days to make sure she could use the bathroom on her own and eat to keep up her strength, and then they would start with the physical part of her treatment.

Kian felt some relief in the news; it gave him a few days to compose himself and figure out a way to work with Adalyn Phillips without getting so caught up in "her." Everything about her intrigued him and the woman hadn't even said a full word to him yet. Being this close to a patient was something Kian had never experienced before. He knew why, but that didn't make it any easier to accept. And he certainly couldn't be honest with Adalyn Phillips about it.

Addy was tired. Sweat was pouring off of her brow as she was asked to pick up a tennis ball, first with her left hand, then her right hand. Such a simple task, in her mind, but it was almost torturous, physically speaking.

She'd had three days of speech therapy, with her therapist helping her to cope with "tricks" in figuring out how to speak. She'd managed to say "hi, bye, and mom," and she felt really behind, like she was moving too slowly.

Today, Kian showed up to give her the first in a series of tests to see what her muscles remembered. At least that's what he told her. From what she could see, the damn things couldn't remember much. Huffing out a breath, she dropped the tennis ball.

Watching Adalyn, Kian could see her frustration. He'd worked with a lot of patients recovering from strokes or heart attacks, and it was deeply upsetting when your body betrayed you. "Good job," He said brightly, and gained a glare from Adalyn in response. "I mean it," He said a little more sternly, "Yer muscles weren't required to be workin for a long time; do ya think they'll just do your bidding now?"

Looking up, Adalyn nodded yes.

Her adamancy made him laugh. "Oh, yer a spitfire now, aren't ya?" He asked rhetorically.

Again, Adalyn nodded yes.

"Oh, I could see that in ya, right off," Kian said. "Just want the world to do yer biddin, is that right?"

Now she was genuinely smiling, and, once again, nodded yes.

Nodding himself, Kian responded, "Well, let's just see what we'll be doin to make that a reality for ya now."

Feeling better, emotionally, Adalyn turned to look at the tennis ball, and picked it up again with her right hand. And, when she was able to lift it a good 3 inches off the table, she smiled smugly at Kian.

    Evelyn Phillips placed the phone call she'd been dreading since the moment that her sweet daughter woke up. Dialing the number given to her, she patiently waited for the line to connect. When there was finally a "Hello," at the other end, she said, "Tom, this is Evelyn Phillips."

    Tom Dickson stopped midstride. He was walking out to his car from his house, on his way to work. He asked coolly, "What can I help you with Mrs. Phillips?"

    Even after three years, Evelyn felt the cold sting of anger slice through her. "I'm only calling to tell you that Adalyn woke up," She rushed the words, not wanting to spend any more time than absolutely necessary on the phone with this man.

    "What?" Tom asked, shocked. He headed back toward the house, stopping just outside the front door, and asked her, "When?"

    She didn't feel that Tom Dickson had any right to get any information about Addy, but her husband, and even Dr. Cooper suggested that they address this so Addy could get closure and start to move on. For her, it was still 2012 and she was about to marry this man. To Evelyn, he was the devil incarnate and she wanted to spare her daughter from even having one thought of him in her head. "About four days ago," She answered matter-of-factly.

Appalled, Tom asked, "And you're just now contacting me?"

Anger, hot and sharp traveled up Evelyn's body, and exited in the form of words, "YOU lost that right to know anything about her when you did what you did!" She screamed into the phone.

Doug Phillips took the phone from his wife, and walked into the next room.

Evelyn could only hear the muted sounds of him speaking, not the actual words, and she was relieved. She should have known she wouldn't be able to hold her temper when speaking to Addy's ex-fiancé, but she wanted to make the call anyway.

After hanging up the phone, Doug walked out onto the porch, where his wife was sitting, and looking out into nothing. "Are you okay?" He asked her as he sat down beside her. They'd decided to go back home, for a day or two, to make sure everything was okay, and make calls to let loved ones know that Addy was awake.

They lived in the small town of Alvin, Texas so word would travel fast. With Addy's celebrity status, it wouldn't take long for Tom's family to learn of the news. If they told him first, they felt it would be better to ensure that he left Adalyn alone.

Looking over at her, still handsome, husband, Evelyn answered, "I'm not real happy with my tone, but I'm okay."

Smiling, because he always knew how logical his wife could be when speaking about her own actions, Doug said, "I figured you'd beat yourself up over that, although he deserved it, pompous ass that he is."

Evelyn was so shocked by her husband's words that she broke out into laughter.

"Making you smile, is my goal every single day," Doug said to his wife.

Cupping her husband's face in her hands, Evelyn leaned over to kiss him, "Oh, you do, my love."

They sat there, Doug holding Evelyn on the bench, for a few minutes, just enjoying their time together, when Doug spoke again, "He wants to see her."

The peace she was just feeling left Evelyn's body in seconds, she jumped up and started pacing. "I don't want him to see her!" She started crying, "He doesn't deserve to get off this easy, Doug."

Nodding in agreement, Doug responded, "I am with you on that Evie," he used his nickname for her in the hopes it would calm her, "but she's got to be wondering, and its better she finds out the truth now."

Tears were streaming down her face as Evelyn paced the length of the porch. The heat of the day hadn't quite permeated the air yet, so the ceiling fans kept it cool. She looked out at their yard, the one they hoped would be teeming with grandkids by now, and felt only loss. "This is his fault!" She shouted, and turned away from her husband, wrapping her arms around herself.

Doug stood and moved behind her, circling her with his arms in an effort to comfort. He'd come to terms with his own demons a couple of years earlier, so it was only slightly easier for him to accept the unfairness of the situation. "It's not all his fault," He said softly into his wife's ear.

Evelyn shook her head, and jerked out of her husband's arms. "Yes," She turned around to face him, "it is."

Leaving the porch, knowing that his wife needed time to absorb all of the things that were about to happen, Doug went inside. He'd do anything to take away the pain he knew his daughter was feeling, was about to go through, and the pain his wife still carried with her. He just had to hope that his faith and love would be enough to get them all through this.

Kian was making notes on his laptop after his session with Adalyn. She was exhausted, he could see it, but she was tough, and tried to put on a tough front. He admired her strength, and knew she would need to draw on that strength in the weeks and months to come.

"Mar..marr," Adalyn tried to say the word, but couldn't, so she pointed to his ring finger.

"Married?" Kian offered to her, and smiled when she nodded. After he saved his work on the laptop, he looked over at her, "I'm thinkin that there's no woman in the world who would want all the trouble that I am."

Giggling, Adalyn shook her head no. She didn't agree.

Pretending to think really hard, Kian pursed his lips, then said, "Well, there was this pretty little cailin, I mean girl, but she felt I was just too much man for her."

Exaggerating the act of fanning herself, Adalyn smiled.

"I'm thinkin that you believe I'm givin you a little blarney aren't ya?" Kian asked her.

Adalyn answered him, "Yyyess." It took a little bit for her to pronounce the word, but she got it out, and was proud of herself for doing so.

Smiling widely, Kian said, "That's my girl," and reached over to squeeze Adalyn's hand.

Feeling his touch made Addy's cheeks flush. She couldn't understand her reaction to him, only that she seemed to be unable to control it. Luckily, Nurse Janice came in to check her vitals so he let go of her hand, and she was able to calm herself down.

After Kian left, Adalyn sat on her bed, and waited for the nurse to come in and help her get cleaned up. The frustration at having to wait for someone to "help" you go to the bathroom or even brush your teeth aggravated her. These moments, when she was alone were the worst. The doubts and fears crept into her mind and haunted her.

Chapter 6

The next morning, Addy smiled wide when her parents came into her room. "Mom, Dad," She said with confidence, and was so pleased with their reaction to her words.

"Wow," Doug said to his daughter, "Your pronunciation is better."

Nodding, Adalyn, took a breath, and tried to speak, "I.....am.....be....tter."

Evelyn started crying. These little victories were so precious to her. "You are!" She answered her daughter, excitedly.

Dr. Cooper came in a few minutes later, and talked with the three of them. He started with her speech assessment, "The pathologist has gone over a couple of things with Adalyn and we feel that she'll gain back most of her speech. Finding the words, she wants may be her biggest struggle. We equate it to looking through a dictionary but not sure how to spell the word, so you don't really know where to look first. She has to re-train her brain to recall what the words are and re-file them."

Doug asked him, "How long do you think she'll be in speech therapy?"

"You know we can't guarantee anything," He saw them all nod, then continued, "but we think about a year."

It wasn't as bad as Doug feared. Then he asked, "What about the physical therapy?"

Checking over Adalyn's chart, Dr. Cooper read something then set it down. "I've looked over what Dr. Tillman is saying and what I discussed with Kian after Adalyn's last two sessions," He smiled, "And we feel that her muscle memory is good, and it certainly doesn't hurt that she's determined."

Evelyn smiled, "Yes, she is that."

Addy snorted, and they all laughed.

"But, the really exciting news," He said while looking at Adalyn, "is that you'll be able to do most of your rehab while at home."

'Home,' Addy ran the word through her mind a few times. "Wh...e....e," She tried to say.

Doug squeezed his daughter's hand, "She'll be coming home with us and staying there."

Confused, Adalyn nodded. She wanted to know what happened to Tommy and to her apartment near Dallas. For now, though, knowing that she wouldn't need to be in the hospital forever, was the best news.

"How long do you think she'll be here?" Evelyn asked Dr. Cooper.

Picking up Adalyn's chart, Dr. Cooper answered, "We will be running EEG's about every two days, to ensure there's no change in her brain waves, but we think she'll be here another month or so, then she can go home." He added, "We'll want her to come in to the office every two weeks for the first 6-8 weeks she's home, and then we'll play it by ear after that."

The news was such a Blessing; Evelyn looked over at her husband, and smiled. She knew he was thinking the exact same thing. "Okay," She answered Dr. Cooper.

Once Dr. Cooper left, Adalyn turned to hug her parents. She was happy that she would not be in the hospital, but still, the questions she was unable to ask jumbled up her mind.

"Sweetheart," Her father said, smiling, "we were able to get ahold of Tom."

Curious, Addy replied, "Yesss."

Glancing at his wife, Doug could see her distress, but he wouldn't allow himself to feel that way, not when their daughter's health was being restored. He turned back to Addy, and said, "He's going to come and see you."

Nodding, while smiling, Adalyn was happy and not happy at the same time. The problem was, she had absolutely no idea why she felt that way.

Her mother took Adalyn into her arms, and whispered, "It will all be okay, Dad and I promise," and Addy believed her.

Evelyn and Doug were at the center as early as they were allowed to be the next morning. Addy was just waking up and Evelyn helped her get to the bathroom to start getting ready. They knew today was the day that Tommy was supposed to "stop by" but they hadn't told Addy yet.

As Evelyn assisted Addy with using the toilet, then washing her hands, she wondered how her daughter would handle what was to come. She put the toothpaste on the toothbrush and helped Addy get it up to her mouth. She could make the motion of brushing her teeth without too much help. Evelyn was thankful for each little victory. If that meant brushing teeth, or brushing hair, or even saying "Mom," was better than living in the limbo they'd had for the last three years.

After turning on the shower, Evelyn stood by while Adalyn showered.

Addy preferred to at least try to do it on her own. Not that she didn't appreciate her mom's hovering, just in case, but she wanted to work on independence. Now that she was "awake," there seemed to be a constant barrage of people coming in and out of her room. Between therapists, her parents, doctors, nurses, and visitors, she rarely got any time to herself. A few minutes in the shower, under the hot water, felt like heaven. She grabbed the scrubber that had a handle, so she didn't have to stretch too far in order to reach her limbs, and put soap on it.

Her body looked so different than she remembered it. She'd always been naturally prone to being on the thin side, which was probably why she'd gotten into modeling in the first place. Now, she looked really frail. Her limbs were thin as sticks with very little muscle mass. Leaning on the bars in the shower, she managed to get the shampoo in, but lacked the strength to keep standing. "Mom," She said, and waited for Evelyn to peek around the end of the shower curtain. Pointing to the shower chair, Addy thanked her mother with a smile as she scooted it over and guided Addy into it. "Thanks," She managed, and smiled because it was a word she had tripped up on before.

"You're welcome, baby," Evelyn said, feeling the sting of tears of joy in her eyes. Without asking, she helped Addy put her head back so she could rinse out the shampoo, then proceeded to put on the conditioner, and rinse that out too.

Once Adalyn was bathed, dressed, and primped, as much as one could be in a rehabilitation center, she let her mom help her back to bed. These little "trips" just zapped her strength and she needed a nap.

Drifting off, she thought she saw someone come into her room, but couldn't keep her eyes open long enough to see who it was.

Tommy Dickson came into Adalyn's room, and he wasn't alone. Once Evelyn saw him, and his company, she stood up and started for them. "What do you think you're doing?" She asked in a sharp whisper.

Doug was up, and by her side in a moment. "Maybe now's not the best time."

Upset by their words, Tommy retorted, "You know, we drove a long way to see her."

Just his mere presence made Evelyn's blood boil. When he used that tone, the one of entitlement, she wanted to go at him like a wild animal. "You listen here," She said accusingly, and allowed her husband to guide them all outside and into the hallway.

"I'm going to see her," Tommy said loudly.

Kian was walking down the hall when he saw the man and woman standing with the Phillips'. It was easy to see that there was no warm welcome between the couples. Seeing as it wasn't his business, but stepping forward anyway, Kian asked Mr. and Mrs. Phillips, "Is there a problem here?"

Turning toward this candy striper, Tommy looked insulted, "Listen here, you just mind your own business and go clean a bed pan or something."

"Tommy," The woman with him said, clearly embarrassed by his tone.

Stepping between the Phillips' and the other two people, Kian said in a low, but intense voice, "I'd be watching what you say there ye gowl."

"What the hell are you saying?" Tommy asked loudly, as if he were trying to bully Kian.

Evelyn happened to turn around, and saw that their loud altercation had managed to wake up Adalyn. "Addy," She said, and walked back in the room.

Doug followed his wife, but Kian stood between Tommy and the other woman, saying, "You best be on yer best behavior or you'll be wearin a bed pan as I throw yer arse out of here."

Pushing past Kian, Tommy gave him only an annoyed glance. The woman with him, said, "I'm sorry," in a quiet tone.

Bracing herself, Evelyn watched the play of emotions on her daughter's face. At first, she saw a smile fill Addy's face, but then, when Addy noticed that Tommy was walking in with her best friend, Jeni, the smile faded.

"Hello Adalyn," Tommy said. He didn't even smile. "Your parents called to tell us you were awake, and we're so relieved," He said the words coldly, as if he were talking about the weather, and wrapped his arm around Jeni's shoulders.

Adalyn watched, as her fiancé walked in with her best friend. At first, she was happy, but the situation revealed itself, a dark shadow settled itself over her body. Looking down, she noticed the baby bump Jeni wore, and her breath hitched.

"Yes," Tommy announced, "We're married and expecting our first child."

Doug stepped forward, "You know, if you're just going to be an ass, you should go."

Evelyn, shocked by her husband's choice of words, but proud of him for saying what she was thinking, just nodded and sat down next to Addy.

Jeni turned to Tommy, and said, "Let's go, Tommy."

"Why isn't she saying anything?" Tommy demanded, and pointed toward Adalyn. "She knows what happened! Why not confront us now?"

Grabbing this idiot by the scruff of his neck, and ignoring his, "Hey, you can't manhandle me," Kian jerked the man out of Adalyn's room, and didn't stop until he had him outside the building. A worried looking Jeni followed them.

As Kian pushed this inconsiderate arse outside, he yelled, "She can't talk, you idiot, because of her head injury, and she can't confront you because she doesn't remember the accident." He was yelling, but didn't care, "And if you had one shred of decency inside of your narcissistic body, you'd have some damn compassion." He turned to Jeni, and said, "I feel sorry for you and the babe, if he's the father." Without waiting for them to respond, Kian went inside.

Doug met him in the hallway, outside of Adalyn's room. "Thank you, Kian," He said, extending his hand to shake Kian's.

Shaking his head, Kian replied, "It was my pleasure, sir," and shook Mr. Phillips' hand. "Is he really that daft?" He asked the older man.

"I'm afraid so," Doug answered. He looked toward Adalyn's room, and said, "She's so confused, but a few of her questions are now answered."

Feeling a little uncomfortable, but curious, Kian asked, "What did he mean by, 'Why isn't she confronting us?'"

Worried about his daughter, and knowing Kian wouldn't hurt her, Doug felt giving the young man an explanation wouldn't hurt, so he responded, "The day of the accident, she'd gone over to Tommy's house, as a surprise, and found him and Jeni in bed together." He hated even thinking about what his little girl must have gone through, "She was so upset, we figured that was why she had the accident, crying or something, and running off the road."

"Oh," Kian answered. He'd never asked about the story before. Knowing this information confused him. He'd have to chew on this information for a while.

The two men went back in the room. Addy turned and said, "Dad," and "Kian," very clearly.

"Well, now yer talking like nobody's business," Kian said with a smile. "I got that lout outta here for ya, and I don't think he'll be stickin his nose in yer business anymore."

Adalyn smiled again, and said, "My he.....ro."

Kian blushed, and Doug clapped him on the back. "Look at that," He said to Kian, "She's already got you pegged."

If things had been different, Kian would have loved to take on the job of "hero," but he now had a few more pieces of the puzzle and he wasn't so sure.

Chapter 7

The next few weeks were miraculous, as far as Kian was concerned. Adalyn Phillips surpassed everyone's expectations, and was well on her way to recovery. Sometimes, he half thought that she'd never been in a coma.

They did therapy every day, doing a variety of exercises to strengthen her major muscle groups, and then smaller, more intense skills that worked on her fine motor coordination. The sessions took a toll on her, he could see that for sure.

By the end of their time together, Adalyn was covered in sweat. Kian admired her stamina, she pushed herself so hard; grim determination constantly set in her features. She was determined to make progress, and she did.

"Good job," Kian told her, as they finished up their last exercise for the day.

Adalyn looked at him, the look in her eyes, one of anger; but for only a brief second, before she smiled and her face was transformed into relaxation. "Thank you," She said, her words stilted, but much smoother, as she spoke.

He nodded, and handed her a towel. She was able to take it from him, but her hands simply held it in her lap. Taking it from her, he brought the towel up and wiped her brow first, then moved down to wipe the sweat from her neck.

The sensation of Kian touching her, even with the towel as a buffer, did funny things to Addy's skin. She felt a warmth that had nothing to do with physical exertion, travel through her belly. It snuck up on her, this feeling of awareness. She looked down at her hands, praying they would work the way she wanted them to.

Evelyn came into the room, and stopped. She saw Kian gently using a towel to help wipe the perspiration off of Addy's face and neck. Even though it was a sweet thing to do, the act itself wasn't what stopped her, it was the look on Kian's face that brought Evelyn to a standstill. There was something there, certainly nothing negative, but it was intense, maybe protective, the way he watched her daughter. Clearing her throat, to announce her presence, Evelyn asked, "How did it go today?"

Kian smiled at Mrs. Phillips, and answered, "We've got quite a savage fighter, here," he nodded to Adalyn.

Smiling back, Evelyn responded, "I have no doubt about that."

Adalyn smiled at her mom. "Hi," She said, and lifted her hand up a few inches in a small wave.

"Are you ready to shower now, sweetheart?" Evelyn asked her daughter.

Nodding, Adalyn looked back at Kian, and mumbled, "Bye," before letting her mom help her off to the bathroom.

Kian stared after them, wondering if he'd done something wrong. Adalyn looked uncomfortable with him, and she seemed really relieved when her mom came in. He made a mental note to ask her about it.

Adalyn spent the afternoon with her speech therapist. She could manage a few short sentences now, but the flow of her speaking was still choppy most of the time. It frustrated her, but she was thankful for being awake.

At night, when everyone was gone, and she was alone, she would feel the fear sneak up on her. The fear that if she went to sleep, she wouldn't wake up again.

She knew there were things her parents kept from her too, but she was afraid to ask the questions.

Between all the worries, Addy began to feel suffocated with her own emotions. The next day, when Kian came into her room, she hadn't even gotten dressed.

"Good morning," Kian said to Adalyn, and noticed she didn't even look his way in acknowledgement. Without missing a beat, he announced, "We're going to begin walking today, I'm going to take ya down to the physical therapy room, and we'll get you up and goin." Still, he received no answer. Getting worried, Kian walked around the bed until he was standing in Adalyn's direct line of sight. "What's this all about?" He murmured, trying to be sweet.

Adalyn didn't want his kindness, and shouted back, "Go!"

Her tone, and the word itself, surprised Kian. "Adalyn," He started to say, when she shouted again, "GO!"

Without a word, Kian nodded, picked up his gear, and left the room.

The same thing happened later that day, when Adalyn's speech therapist came in for her daily session. A few minutes later, the woman came out, almost in tears from Adalyn's refusal to cooperate.

Nurse Suzie called Dr. Cooper, and explained the situation. He nodded to her, and went into Adalyn's room. Closing the door behind him, he didn't say anything, just grabbed a chair and pulled it up to the side of Adalyn's bed.

"Go!" She yelled at him.

Sitting there, Dr. Cooper asked her, "Why?"

She glared at him, and managed to say, "I want be alone."

Again, Dr. Cooper asked her, "Why?"

Angry at him, and everyone, Adalyn raised her hand to strike him. She was still slow and weak so he easily grabbed her arm to stop her motion. "You're mad," He stated matter-of-factly.

Adalyn nodded.

"You're mad because this is all so new, and scary, and no one will leave you alone, and you're afraid to be left alone, right?" He asked her in a soft tone.

Tears started falling down Addy's cheeks, and she nodded.

Understanding, partially due to a colleague's advice, and reading up on this kind of rehabilitation, Dr. Cooper was warned that this might happen. "Do you want a break for a couple of days?" He asked her.

She nodded again, "I am scared," she mumbled.

Putting her arm down, and patting her hand, Dr. Cooper said, "I'll bet you are. This is all so confusing, and you've had a lot to absorb. I'll tell you what," He suggested, "I'm going to start you on an anxiety medication to keep you calmer, and you'll probably get more sleep, and I'll bet you'll start to feel better."

"Okay," Adalyn answered, "Go," she added.

Trying not to smile, Dr. Cooper stood, and nodded in agreement to her.

When her parents showed up a few hours later, Dr. Cooper met with them in his office.

"Is everything okay?" Evelyn Phillips asked, worry lacing her words.

Dr. Cooper nodded, "Yes," he motioned for them to sit down, "It's more of a psychological issue right now." He sat down, and continued, "She's refusing to work with her therapists."

Doug leaned forward, "So what does that mean?" He asked.

"It means," Dr. Cooper explained, "That Adalyn is going through a normal adjustment period for her condition. She's scared, confused, frustrated that her body isn't doing what her mind is telling it, and she has to adjust to a new reality." He smiled reassuringly, "Really, we've all had 3 years to adjust while she's only had three and a half weeks."

Evelyn nodded in understanding, "So what now?" She asked him.

Leaning forward, Dr. Cooper placed his hands together on his desk, and said, "Well, I'm placing her on an anxiety medication and an anti-depressant. We're discontinuing her therapy sessions for a couple of days only," He didn't want the Phillips' to think he was giving up, "And then we'll start up again and, hopefully, Adalyn will be more receptive."

"But, this is normal?" Doug asked the doctor.

Shaking his head side to side, Dr. Cooper replied, "Let's face it, nothing she's going through is "normal." I just think we've got to address each step forward and try to prevent the steps backward."

Both Evelyn and Doug nodded in agreement. They left Dr. Cooper's office and went down the hall to Adalyn's room. She was lying in bed, just as she had been all day. Nurse Suzie was coming out of the room, and gave them a look of pity.

Evelyn sat down next to her daughter, and smiled, "Hi sweetie."

Adalyn gave her mother a brief glance, then turned her head to look out the window.

"Addy?" Doug Phillips addressed his daughter from the other side of the bed.

Not moving, Addy stayed in the exact same place, and didn't move.

Getting upset, Doug Phillips did something he hadn't had to do for a very long time, where his daughter was concerned anyway, he raised his voice. "Adalyn Rose Phillips, you will not ignore your mother, or me, and you will stop this childish behavior right now."

Finally turning her head, Adalyn looked at her father. She was certainly surprised by his tone, but she couldn't say she blamed him. All day, she'd sunk lower and lower into this abyss of uncertainty and fear. "I'm sorry, Dad," She said to him.

Evelyn started crying, and grabbed her daughter's hand, squeezing it lightly. "Oh sweetheart, we know this is hell on you," She let the tears fall, not caring how she looked, "We're just grateful to have you back."

"I know, Mom," Addy answered, letting her own tears fall.

Doug moved forward and sat down on the bed with his wife and daughter. "We love you, and we won't let you just wither away because we are here for you," He pointed out into the hall, "The doctors and nurses and therapists are here for you."

Feeling ashamed that she'd been such a bitch to both Kian and Sheri, her therapists, Addy just nodded.

Evelyn spoke up, "So, now what are we going to do with your days off of therapy?"

Turning back toward the window, Addy said, "Outside."

Her parents smiled at one another. They would do whatever they could to help their daughter. Even if it meant "breaking out" of the rehab center for a few hours.

Doug left the room and went out to the nurse's station. He asked the nursing assistant, he thought her name was Julie, if he could get a wheelchair. She left, and came back with a one a few minutes later.

While her husband was out getting transportation, Evelyn helped her daughter get cleaned up and dressed. Sometimes, it was still a shock to see how thin Adalyn looked. A friend had forwarded a pic of Addy, with a friend, that was taken just a few weeks before the accident. They were at some birthday party and Addy looked so happy and healthy.

Evelyn studied the picture before they left to visit Addy here, and sighed thinking of the time they lost. Now wasn't the time to be worrisome though, they should just be rejoicing in the fact that they had Addy back, and she was living again, not just "existing."

Doug was waiting for them, as soon as they finished in the bathroom. "Let's go," He said in a whisper, as if they were doing something they shouldn't.

Adalyn sat down in the wheelchair, and lifted her feet so her mother could put down the foot rests. She was all set when her father spun the chair around so fast, she started to giggle. They were off then, going quickly down the hall, and outside the building.

Dr. Cooper stood around the corner, out of sight of the threesome, and smiled as the nurses looked at him. If getting out of here would help Adalyn Phillips recover, then that's what they would do. He turned around and headed back to his office, smiling the whole way.

As the door opened, and Doug pushed his daughter outside, into the afternoon air, he could literally feel her worries lighten. Her shoulders loosened, and she lifted her face upward so the sun was shining on it. Seeing her like this, brought back memories of her childhood and he wanted to weep for the joy of this moment. Thank the Lord that Addy was given back to them.

Addy sat quietly as her parents navigated her wheelchair down the walkway from the rehabilitation center. It wound around the building and out through a park-like setting. There were benches set strategically so that people could sit and visit, or rest if they were trying to regain their strength. Addy wondered when she would be one of those people, walking along the path. Remembering that Kian came in this morning, ready to help her try to regain that part of herself back, she felt remorse.

Maybe the fear she was feeling was somewhat unfounded. Maybe she just needed to find her faith and work on that for a while. As her parents walked with her in the warm afternoon, she tried to think of what she would say to Kian the next time she saw him.

Chapter 8

Kian received an email later that day, from Dr. Tillman, who'd gotten a request from Dr. Cooper to give Ms. Phillips a few days to rest and be put on some different medications before they continued her therapy sessions. Kian noted that her speech therapist was also included in the request. For some reason, seeing that it wasn't just him, made him feel a little better.

If he were Adalyn Phillips, he was pretty sure he'd have gone round the bend and wore a puss, sulky face, all the time. The frustration of not being able to speak yer mind must be awful.

"Hi, Kian," His neighbor, Missy, said as she passed him on the sidewalk.

Kian smiled out of habit, and returned, "Hello to ya as well." She kept going, looking down, and Kian hoped she found herself before her shyness kept her down and about.

He was about halfway up the stairs to his apartment, when Kian heard Missy ask, "Would you like to go out sometime?"

Shocked by her question, Kian turned around slowly. She was a sweet girl and he felt that she'd be a nice date, so he said, "Sure, ya just give me a shout out."

Missy nodded, blushing, and turned to hurry toward the parking lot.

As Kian opened the door to his apartment, he wondered if he was just attracted to the odd girls. His thoughts immediately flew back to Adalyn Phillips. She certainly wasn't odd. Not in the conventional way, at least. Her beauty was inside as well as outside, but she needed help in rediscovering who that was after what she'd been through.

After grabbing something to eat from his sorry excuse for a kitchen, Kian sat down on the sofa and stared at the television. He needed to get to the gym, or call a friend, or get out and do something, yet he just sat there, thinking about Adalyn Phillips.

The story her father told him, about how they suspected the accident happened; it threw him emotionally. He wondered........if knowing something, that you couldn't do anything about now anyway, and didn't make a difference to others at this point.....was it worth speaking up about? That was the question he would need to consider long and hard. And, it was a question that he certainly wouldn't find the answer to anytime soon.

The next morning, Adalyn met with a psychologist, per Dr. Cooper's orders. Christie, as she requested Adalyn call her, was kind and quiet. "So," She began, as they sat down together in the lounge area, "Dr. Cooper said you're having a bit of trouble adjusting to everything."

Talk about an understatement, Addy thought to herself. "Well," She said slowly, "tough to fi...gure it out."

"I see," Christie said, "and I realize that communicating is a little frustrating so we can do whatever you like, write, type, or talk about it."

It didn't occur to Adalyn to use anything other than her voice. "Type," She answered, and sat there waiting.

Christie pulled out a tablet, set it to a typewriter looking app, and gave both the tablet and the stylus to Adalyn. She used another stylus to show Adalyn what to do.

Smiling, Christie asked, "Let's try this, okay?"

Adalyn nodded.

Looking at her pen and paper, Christie asked, "So do you feel down about waking up and not having things as you remember them?"

Addy pushed the buttons, then turned the screen so Christie could see it.....*YES*.

Nodding, Christie wrote down something, and asked Adalyn, "So, do you feel different about yourself?"

Not needing to type, Addy just pointed at the screen again, and nodded.

"How?" Christie asked.

It took Adalyn a few minutes to think about her answer, and then she started "typing" on the screen. Finally, she turned it around for Christie to read……..*I feel like I'm stuck in what my family thinks I was. I'm no longer a model, I'm disabled.*

Christie shook her head, "You're not disabled, Adalyn." She smiled, and tried to be encouraging, "You're just re-learning the things you need in order to be productive again."

Adalyn typed and turned the screen around……*I don't want to be a model anymore, I want to do something else.*

Nodding, Christie returned, "You can do whatever you want to do."

Thinking about the words, Addy wondered, for the first time, what exactly she wanted to do, rather than what she didn't.

They talked for another hour and a half, since it was slow going with Adalyn having to type her answers. Christie spoke to Dr. Cooper, who said he would ask Adalyn's parents to get her a tablet so she could communicate easier with everyone else.

When Addy got back to her room, she actually did feel better. Christie wasn't going to judge her decisions, she wasn't there to tell her what to do, and she was only there to listen. It wasn't until now that Adalyn realized how much she'd needed that.

There were things she could remember with perfect clarity; walking the runway at fashion shows, driving in her car, her apartment, her childhood, and even what she was planning for her wedding. And then there were gaps......like what she was doing before the accident. When Tommy came to see her, and was an ass; it didn't even bother her, except how much his presence bothered her parents. Seeing Jeni with him, obviously pregnant, and with a ring on her finger, didn't even bother Addy that much. It was sad to know that too. If Tommy being gone and losing her best friend didn't bother her, then what was wrong with her?

There were still a million questions to ask her parents, so she was excited to get the tablet, if possible.

The appointments with Christie would be good for her, Addy could understand that, and she would do everything she could to get out of here, and back on her own two feet. There was a lot of guilt flying around, and she didn't like it.

Evelyn Phillips came into her daughter's room, and sensed a difference. Scanning the room, she didn't notice anything different, Addy was sleeping peacefully, but she felt something. Walking over to Addy's bed, she sat down and took her daughter's hand into her own.

Addy stirred, and opened her eyes. She smiled, and said, "Hi, Mom," in a sleepy voice. She hated needing to take naps during the day, but it was a necessity right now.

"Hi, daughter," Evelyn returned, with a smile. "How was your appointment with Christie?" She wasn't sure how far to push her daughter, but she was curious, and wanted to help in any way possible.

Sitting up, Adalyn stretched, then settled back down. "It... was good," She tried to formulate the words, "I need a....ta....let."

"A tablet?" Evelyn asked. She smiled when Addy nodded, then reached down into her bag and produced a tablet. Just seeing her daughter's eyes light up was an enormous emotional boost. "Christie called me too, and suggested we try it." She pushed the power button, "And, she told me which app to get so you could type."

Addy waited for her mother to turn on the tablet, and turn it to the appropriate page. When she held it in her hands, Addy felt lighter, emotionally. Maybe because it wouldn't be as frustrating to type as it was to actually say the words out loud. She tapped the screen with her fingers, and typed, *Hi mom.*

Laughing, Evelyn nodded her approval. Then, she asked Adalyn, "How are you feeling, really?"

Tapping on the screen again, Addy took a few minutes to respond, then she handed the tablet to her mom. It said, *I'm scared and sad that you and dad had to go through this.*

Tears started down Evelyn's cheeks, "Oh sweetie," she squeezed Adalyn's hand to reassure her, "we're just so thankful we got you back."

Addy typed, *Did I almost die?* She knew the question would be hard for her mother, but she wanted to know the truth.

Evelyn read the tablet, and nodded. "I think both Daddy and I thought you would, yes." She grabbed a tissue from her purse and dabbed her eyes, before continuing, "Then, they saw that you were breathing on your own, and took you off the ventilator." She waited for Adalyn to nod, and went on with, "They said you could be like that forever, so, after two years, we had you moved down here so you could be closer to us."

Why didn't you move me sooner? Addy typed.

Sighing, Evelyn told her, "Addy, there was a very big financial fight between us and Tommy." She didn't want to completely paint Addy's ex-fiancé as a monster, but he really was. "Your medical expenses were coming out of your own accounts because you were financially able to handle what your insurance couldn't." Evelyn took a breath. "Well, you had put Tommy on your account because you were getting married, and when he found out, he wanted the money to stop coming out of that account." She started crying again, "He said it was his."

No wonder she didn't feel anything for that man? Addy knew he was a jerk, could perfectly see it now, and so why did she still want to marry him back then? Typing back to her mom, she wrote, *None of that money was his. Im so sorry he was an ass.*

Adalyn's use of the profanity made Evelyn chuckle. She looked at her daughter, and said, "Baby, if I could shield you from all of this I would."

Even if it hurt, which Addy knew it would, it all needed to be done. *Mom, I can take it. Better to know now than later.*

Evelyn was so proud of her little girl. Not everyone could possess the strength Adalyn had shown. And knowing there was still more to overcome, she worried constantly about her daughter. "I know you can. I'm just being a worried mommy."

Typing, Adalyn smiled, and turned the tablet so her mother could see it, *I'm glad to have you and dad.*

As if summoned, Doug Phillips came into the room, a big smile on his face. "How are my two favorite ladies today?" He asked as he leaned down to kiss Adalyn on the forehead.

Smiling, Addy set the tablet on her lap and typed, *Much easier now that I can talk better.*

Doug read the words, and chuckled. It's as if miracles just happened every day with his little girl. "Good, now you can tell us what's going on and spread gossip, like the other patients."

Addy laughed. It sounded strange, her own laugh, to her ears. It was if someone else was making the noise. She wanted to laugh, she wanted to be free, and she wanted to get out of this place.

Two days later, Kian came back to the rehabilitation center to work with Adalyn Phillips. He was worried that she would still be down, like she was the last time he was here. As his mother always told him, "be leery when a woman is in a sour mood." He went into her room cautiously. And he stopped when he saw her. She was standing at the window, surrounded by the light of the sunny day, and smiling. If Kian didn't know better, he'd swear on all that was Holy that this wasn't the same lass. "Well, a fine sight yer makin this glorious morning," He said to her.

At the sound of Kian's voice, Adalyn looked up from her tablet. Her mother had shown her how to get onto YouTube so she was really into watching funny videos. Mostly, they consisted of animals and their antics but some were clips from television shows and movies. "Good……mor….ning," She replied to Kian, and wondered why she had that little flutter happen in her chest every time he came into the room.

Kian noticed the smoother tone with her speaking, so that was good. "Are ya ready to work today?" He asked as he set down his bag and table.

Nodding, Adalyn slowly made her way over to the bed, with the help of a walker. Walking was still a little wobbly, but she could see it getting easier with every passing day. She set down the tablet long enough to sit down, then picked it back up, and typed, *I'm sorry I was so mean to you the last time you were here. I am still upset about all of this.*

"I understand, or think I do, what yer goin through," Kian said and handed her back the tablet.

Addy frowned, and typed, *How do you understand?*

He spoke as he worked, it kept his mind from getting too jumbled up with emotion. "Well, me parents, they were in an auto accident and needed physical rehabilitation."

Nodding, Adalyn found herself feeling sad for him. She typed, *Are they doing better now?*

Kian shook his head no, "I'm sorry to say it, they both passed on."

Now Adalyn felt silly for even bringing it up, "I'm....sor..ry," she said.

For some reason, he didn't want her to feel that way, "Nah," he started, "They lived a grand life, the two of them together."

Even with her mind a bit jumbled, Adalyn knew that he was playing it off and it was his place to choose to do that. She just didn't want any sadness today. Typing, she smiled, *I promise I'll be a good girl and do whatever I need to.*

"Oh, sure enough, you'll be cursin me like the devil by the time we're done, but that's just fine," He replied. Motioning for her to move over to the portable bed he set up, he started working on her feet.

As soon as Kian's hands touched her feet, Adalyn felt this warmth move through her body. It was if there was kindling inside of her that finally found the spark it needed to warm. And the smell, she had a vision of palm trees with gentle breezes moving their fronds. "That sm..ell," She said.

"Plumeria," Kian answered, "your mum requested that I use it since you like it so much."

Tears started falling down her cheeks, with waves of emotions flowing through her. Adalyn actually felt her body being wracked with the waves of emotional hurt.

Kian felt the change in her, then saw her crying. Thinking he'd somehow hurt her, he stood up and walked to her side, "Oh, mo milis," he whispered, and took Adalyn into his arms.

Adalyn had no idea what he was saying, only that he was holding her, and it did crazy things to her inside. The tears wouldn't stop and Addy didn't even try to stop them. They needed to be shed, for everything she lost, and to clear her mind for what she needed to do.

Evelyn walked into her daughter's room, and stopped at the doorway. Seeing Kian hold Adalyn the way he was, as if she was the most precious thing in the world, made her heart ache. Doug almost ran into the back of her, and started to say, "What.." when he saw Kian and Addy.

Kian just ran his hand down the back of Adalyn's head, feeling the softness of her hair as it wrapped around his fingers. Her arms were tightly around him, as if she were holding on for dear life, and maybe, to her way of thinking, she was. If this bit of comfort was what he could give her, then he'd be a happier man for having done it. "It's okay," He whispered into her hair.

Leaning away from him, Adalyn looked up into his beautiful green eyes. They made her think of leprechauns and magic; she smiled. "Thank....you," She choked out.

Slowly releasing her, Kian stood up, and replied, "Yer welcome, sweet lass."

Chapter 9

A week later, Kian was in sheer awe of Adalyn Phillips. She did everything he asked of her during their physical therapy sessions, and he knew that took all of her strength. He'd been told, by the nursing staff, that she was doing the exercises in the early evenings as well.

They were currently working with one pound weights to get her arm muscles to work the way she needed them to. "Very fine," He commented, after her third set with her right arm.

"It's hard," Adalyn said, switching the weight over to her left arm.

Smiling, Kian winked at her, and said, "It's supposed to be hard, that way you'll get those wee muscles in better shape."

Taking his words as a challenge, she was sure he meant it that way, Addy gutted it out, and completed the sets. "There," She said when she was done.

Nodding at her, Kian replied, "And a fine job you've done of it."

Since she was resting before the next exercise in their regimen, Addy said, "I love the way you talk." There was only a slight pause between her words now, so she sounded almost normal.

"You'll be makin me blush now," Kian responded, and batted his eyes at her playfully.

Addy laughed. She didn't think the sound of her own laughter was so odd now. And, she noticed that she laughed the most when it was time for her physical rehab, which made no sense since it was the hardest part of her day. The little flutter in her chest, when she saw Kian walk in, was still something she wasn't used to, but it was something she expected and enjoyed.

"Are ya slackin on me now?" Kian asked when Adalyn didn't start her next exercise.

Shaking her head in denial, Adalyn answered, "Sorry, I was think...ing."

Watching her blush, Kian was intrigued. "And what would ya be thinkin about so hard that you can't be focusin on what we're doin here?" He pointed to the weights.

Adalyn answered, "You."

Her honesty both surprised him, and, gave him a jolt of arousal he wasn't expecting. "Me?" He asked her, "And what would you be thinkin about me?"

Looking at Kian, Adalyn picked up the weights and started the next exercise. Now that she'd opened up her mouth, and blabbed like a twelve-year old, she wasn't sure how to explain. "I was think...ing," She started, "that I smile more when you are here."

The words she spoke were like a balm on Kian's emotionally scarred heart. There was a soothing sensation that spread through his chest and gave him a sense of calm. Normally, when a woman flirted with him, and he'd take Adalyn's words as flirtatious, he was more acutely aware. Now, though, he was more.......connected to himself. "Why, I'll be thankin ya for that."

"You are wel...come," Adalyn replied, and continued with the weights to complete the set.

An hour later, when she was physically exhausted, and dripping with sweat, she watched as he picked up his supplies and packed them in his duffle bag. "What have I mis..sed?"

Kian stopped what he was doing, and looked at her, before asking "Missed?"

Adalyn tipped her head, as if studying him. She asked, "What have I miss....ed in the last 3 years?"

That was a loaded question as far as Kian was concerned. What could he tell her? What did she expect him to say? "I guess I'd be askin ya to be a bit more specific about that question," Was his reply.

Sighing, Adalyn geared herself up for speaking. She said, "Did someone find a cure for......can....cer? Was there a great dis..cov...er....y?" She was getting frustrated because there were so many things she wanted to ask and the words were hard to say all at once.

Moving, Kian sat down beside her on the bed, making sure he didn't touch her. He looked solemn when he answered, "There is no cure for cancer, and the only thing I can tell you is that cell phones are smarter, and people usin em, well, they aren't."

His words made Adalyn laugh.

"Now," Kian said, and touched her leg gently, before standing back up, "If I don't get over to Mrs. Wilkins' room, she'll be thinkin I'm cheating on her."

Still smiling, Adalyn nodded. "Okay," She said almost without hesitation. "I'll see you to...morr...ow?" She asked.

Winking at her, before picking up his duffle and his table, Kian replied, "I'll be countin the minutes."

As he walked out of her room, Adalyn wondered if he realized how much of a potent combination his looks, his accent, and his sweetness were on a woman's insides.

Later that day, Evelyn Phillips came into her daughter's room. Her eyes didn't carry the smile she wore on her face, and she knew her daughter knew it too. "Hi, sweetie," She said to Addy, trying to be lighter.

Without preamble, Adalyn asked, "What is it, Mom?"

Evelyn sat down in a chair beside the one Addy was using. She'd taken to sitting in chairs now, as opposed to staying in the hospital bed. It was good to see her doing "normal" things. Now, however, all of the progress she'd made would have a dampener on it. "I'm here to deliver bad news," Evelyn said to her daughter.

Even though Adalyn could see it in her mother's demeanor, to hear the words scared her. "What is it?" She repeated.

"It's Michelle," Evelyn said.

There was a shot of fear that travelled through Adalyn's chest. "What a..bout her?" She asked her mother.

Taking her daughter's hands into her own, Evelyn had difficulty even forming the words. She knew, days earlier, that this was inevitable, and yet, the whole family still hoped, still prayed that things would turn out differently. "You know her heart was weak?" Evelyn asked, and waited for her daughter to respond, before she went on to say, "Well, it just couldn't hold out any longer and she's passed away."

Even though, Adalyn heard the words, she couldn't quite grasp the enormity of them. Instead, her mind wandered back to playing outside at her aunt and uncle's house as children. Discovering hidden treasures in fields or swimming in the backyard pool, or, when they were older, talking about boys. Her cousin was only a year older than Adalyn herself was. And now, she was gone. Suddenly, there was a giant abyss that threatened to swallow Adalyn whole. Tears started down her cheeks, and she let her mother hold her as if she were a young child, instead of an adult.

They sat there, both of them crying, for some time.

When her father showed up later, the three of them had dinner in the dining room, and they talked about Michelle. Evelyn and Doug filling their daughter in on what had been happening during the time Adalyn was in the coma.

"She was so happy that you woke up," Evelyn told her daughter. "She said that God had answered her prayers."

A heavy blanket of guilt covered Adalyn's heart. "How come," She asked her parents, "I woke up, but she cou...ld...n't get a new heart?"

Doug saw that his wife was unable to answer, so he leaned forward, and held Adalyn's hand. "Maybe it was because she had done everything that she needed to do in her life." He smiled reassuringly, "Her parents said that the kids she taught at the local grade school were sending them letters."

Adalyn nodded, and tried to understand, but it didn't seem very fair.

They went back to Addy's room after dinner, and Doug told her, "Well, Dr. Cooper gave us permission to take you out tomorrow. Where would you like to go?"

After looking out the window for weeks, Adalyn should have been excited at the prospect of "getting out," but she just shrugged. "I don't know," She answered her father, still floored by the knowledge that she would never see her cousin again.

When her parents left, Adalyn went through her nightly routine of putting on her night clothes, brushing her hair, and brushing her teeth. Looking in the mirror, she recalled what she would have done, years earlier, before the accident. She would have made sure she ate only what she absolutely needed to survive, then she would have applied creams to her skin, and been worried about any mar in her appearance. Now, she was thrilled just to be up and walking.

As she studied her reflection, she noticed changes, just in the time that she'd been awake. There was more color in her cheeks, and she was finally feeling somewhat balanced, physically speaking. Emotionally, she was still all over the map, but, hopefully Christie would help her to sort out everything she was feeling.

Without prompting, a picture of Kian appeared in her mind, as if she'd conjured him up. He was smiling and, just thinking about him smiling, made Addy smile.

Then, the picture of her cousin, smiling at her while they looked for a wedding dress and bridesmaid dresses, appeared. She'd known since Michelle was 12 years old that her cousin had a heart defect. Over the years, Michelle was the one to cheer Adalyn on as she made her way through the perils of being a fashion model. Addy would call her and they would talk and giggle, late into the night, about some famous person that Adalyn happened to meet. Michelle was never, not for a moment, upset about her medical obstacles, and was always happy to be a teacher.

Personally, Addy thought her cousin was just this side of being a saint. To be "happy" about spending her day with kids was miraculous in Addy's mind. Although, Adalyn always enjoyed the stories her cousin shared about students and their accomplishments. There were times when Adalyn admired her cousin's choice to stay close to her parents and live a quieter life.

Coming back to the present, Adalyn stared at her reflection, and sighed. There would be no more runways, no more fashion shows, and no more of that life. She would need to figure out what she wanted to do now. Luckily, her parents did insist she finish her degree so she had that. Although, she wasn't sure what use a degree in English Literature would get her, she'd just have to figure it out.

Making her way back to her bed, Adalyn wondered if anyone would even hire her. After all, she'd basically been a vegetable for three years. No one in their right mind would hire someone with such a questionable history.

Not willing to be dragged down, once again, into the blackness of depressing thoughts, Adalyn grabbed the remote and turned on the television.

After flipping through the channels, Addy settled on a comedy show about a newly married couple. She needed to laugh, and she needed to do it more than just when Kian was here.

Eventually, Addy fell asleep, the television droning in the background.

She dreamed of walking through a field, her cousin, Michelle was on the far side, and motioning for Adalyn to join her. Starting to run, Addy didn't feel like she was getting anywhere, Michelle seemed far away still. Panic started filling her chest, and she began yelling for her cousin.

Finally, after what seemed like ages, Addy finally got closer to where Michelle was standing. It was a beautiful place, with wild flowers blooming all around. The breeze was light, and gently moved the grasses and tree limbs in their natural dance. Michelle was smiling, and said, "It's okay."

Adalyn woke up, tears filled her eyes.

She got out of bed and went to the window to look out. There was a full moon out, so the area was lit well, even in the middle of the night. Addy jumped when she heard a voice behind her.

"Ms. Phillips," Nurse Suzie said, a frown covering her features, "Are you alright?" She asked Adalyn.

Nodding, Adalyn answered, "Yes," she walked back toward the bed, "I was just drea....ming."

Nurse Suzie smiled warmly, and took Adalyn's wrist into her hand to check her vitals. "Good, I hope."

Frowning herself, Adalyn answered, "You know," she looked up at Suzie intensely, "I'm not sure."

Guiding Ms. Phillips back into the bed, Suzie commented, "You are making such great progress, I think you'll be leaving us soon."

The news made Adalyn nervous. She wanted to start her life again, and was given the chance, but she was safe here. The people here didn't judge her, they just helped her. There were no guarantees that would be the case when she left.

Suzie watched the young woman, and sighed. She clearly had no idea how beautiful she was. Sure, she was a model before her car accident and coma, but the beauty, if it was internal, still showed through. "Don't be afraid, I'm sure you'll be on the cover of some magazines pretty quickly."

Looking up at the nurse, Addy said, "No, I don't do that now."

Surprised, Nurse Suzie nodded, "Well then, you just go out and find a new adventure to pursue."

Adalyn found she liked Nurse Suzie. All of the staff was very nice, but Suzie had a really contagious, positive attitude that made anything seem possible. "I will," Adalyn replied with a smile. She wanted so badly to be excited about finding something new to do, but everything seemed so far away right now. Kind of like her cousin, in the dream.

Chapter 10

Dr. Cooper came into Adalyn's room the next morning, a smile pasted on his face. "Good morning," He said to his miraculous patient. He'd been on the phone with a colleague earlier, and they were discussing Adalyn's progress.

Addy looked up from the book she was reading. Mrs. Wilkins loaned it to her. Her reading was still slower than it was before the accident, but she found it easier as her recovery progressed. It was the story of a woman Marine and how she was falling in love with a guy she thought she couldn't stand. Good story so far. "Good morning," She answered to Dr. Cooper.

He pulled up a chair and sat next to Adalyn. "Well, I've been talking to my colleague in California about you."

Just then, Kian came into the room. He saw Dr. Cooper and stopped immediately. "Uh," He looked at Adalyn, "Should I come back later?" He asked her.

"No," Adalyn answered, "Dr. Cooper was just talking to me."

Nodding, Kian came into the room and started setting up his gear as the doctor talked.

Dr. Cooper smiled, "I think we can start treating you on an out-patient basis starting next week," he said, then added, "We are just so impressed with your recovery, Addy."

Feeling the sharp sting of jealousy fill his chest, Kian tried to ignore the fact that the doctor was using Adalyn's nickname.

"I'm scared," Adalyn responded to the doctor. She wanted to be honest.

Frowning, mostly out of surprise, Dr. Cooper asked her, "What are you afraid of?"

Setting the book down on the small table, beside the chair she was sitting in, Adalyn sighed. "Well, I'm still afraid I'll go to sleep and not wake up."

Dr. Cooper nodded, "I think that's a valid fear, given what's happened to you." He tried to reassure her by patting her hand, "Have you talked about this with Christie?"

Adalyn nodded, "She said the same thing, but I'm still scared." Her voice shook as she spoke now, emotion erupting out of her, "I'm scared of dy...ing."

Her statement had both Dr. Cooper, and Kian stopping in their tracks. Kian didn't care what the doctor did, he walked over and crouched down in front of Adalyn, cupping her face with his hands, "Now there," he whispered, "there'll be no talk of dyin. Yer a beautiful, young woman, with her whole life in front of her. This coma business was just a wee hiccup in your story."

Tears sliding down her cheeks, Adalyn nodded her understanding of his words, but they did little to ease the edge of tension in her soul. The fear was there. She had yet to deal with it fully and, although Christie was helping her, it still stood there, at the edge of her consciousness. She wanted to believe Kian so badly, his eyes pleading that she do just that.

Dr. Cooper cleared his throat, and stood up, saying, "If you need me, Addy, I'll be just down the hall, have the nurses page me." He started to leave the room.

With Kian crouched down in front of her, Adalyn could feel her breathing start to calm down. He had that effect on her, making her feel excited and calm at the same time. It both confused and intrigued her.

Leaving Adalyn's room, Dr. Cooper met up with her parents in the hallway. His face must have looked distraught because Evelyn Phillips rushed over to him, and asked, "What's happened?" He didn't answer, only pointed into the room.

Evelyn and Doug Phillips peeked into their daughter's room and found her in a chair, with Kian in front of her. They couldn't hear what he was saying, but it was plain to see that Adalyn was very intently listening.

Doug turned back around and asked Dr. Cooper, "Is that what it looks like?"

Dr. Cooper shrugged, and answered, "I think so."

Evelyn shook her head, clearly irritated. "How can the two of you be so clueless?" She asked her husband and the doctor. "I knew he was half in love with her even before she woke up."

Doug was concerned, and asked Dr. Cooper, "Is that a violation of doctor-patient relationship?"

Sighing, Dr. Cooper replied, "Not technically, although we do discourage fraternization with patients, Kian is a contractor." He looked back into the room, then at the Phillips, "But he helps her, I've seen it."

"Me too," Evelyn piped in, and looked at her husband, "Don't say anything Douglas, let it go," she directed to him.

Nodding, Doug simply said, "Okay."

"Now," Kian whispered, "Are ya done with the silly talk?"

Giving him a pouty look, Adalyn returned, "It's not sill...y."

He noticed that her speech suffered when she was upset or excited. "It'll be pure nonsense, that's what it is." He cupped her cheek, "Oh, mo milis, there is no reason for you to fear."

Again, he used that term, Adalyn asked him, "What does that mean?"

Taking his hand away from her face, and standing up, Kian answered, "You'd be getting to your therapy now."

Adalyn nodded, but knew that the subject was not dropped. Getting up, under her own power, she walked over to the table he'd set up and got ready to get some working out done.

Evelyn and Doug came into the room then, with Evelyn's smile bright. "Dr. Cooper told us the good news," She said to her daughter, "about you possibly going home next week."

Adalyn nodded at her mother, but concentrated on the exercise Kian asked her to do. Her body didn't respond automatically so she had to concentrate on what she wanted it to do. Right now, that was making a circle in the air with the toe of her shoes.

Doug sat in the chair that Addy vacated, and openly glared at Kian's back. He shot his wife a look of surprise when she elbowed him in the shoulder a few minutes later. Sitting there, he wondered why he shouldn't be leery of any man around his little girl. After all, look what Tommy did?

An hour later, Addy was covered with sweat, but felt good about her exercise program. She could see the approval in Kian's eyes every time she completed a set of the required exercises. He knew which buttons to push though, and that, ticked her off at times. He could goad her into working harder without much effort on his part. "I'm done, are you happy?" She asked him sarcastically.

"I'll be happy when we're sitting in a pub and downing a pint," He answered jokingly.

Sitting up, Adalyn said, "Let's go," and almost laughed at the shocked look on, not only his face, but her parents' faces as well.

Evelyn stood up and walked over to where her daughter was, "I think you might want to shower first, sweetie."

Adalyn blushed. She could only imagine what she must look like after her workout. She got up, with only a little help from her mom, and told Kian, "I guess I'll take a rain….ch….eck."

Kian nodded, "I'll be holdin you to that now," he answered, and started gathering up his supplies.

An hour later, after a nice lunch with her parents in the cafeteria, Adalyn had her session with her therapist, Christie.

"So, is there anything new you'd like to discuss," Christie asked Adalyn.

Sitting there for a couple of minutes, thinking, Adalyn finally answered her, saying, "I feel fun…ny when I'm around Kian, my phy…si….cal ther…apist." The longer words were tricky to get out clearly.

Her eyebrows raised, Christie asked her, "Can you define the word "funny" for me please?"

Adalyn sighed, "Well, I get a tight knot in my stomach," she made a fist in front of her belly to demonstrate, "and I laugh more when he's there."

Nodding in understanding, "Do you think this relationship is healthy?" Christie asked Adalyn.

Getting out her tablet, since what she was going to say was too long for her to get out without stammering, Adalyn wrote… *You realize that nothing in my life is healthy right? I have been asleep for three years. I'm afraid of going to sleep and not waking up, I'm afraid of leaving this place and the safety it provides. I just found out that a woman I respected and loved deeply has died and I never even got to say goodbye. I think having a crush on my physical therapist is about the least of my worries.*

Christie read the paragraph, and started chuckling. "I'll ask for your forgiveness then, Adalyn, I guess it's all about perspective then, isn't it?"

Adalyn nodded. "I'm okay," She said aloud.

Smiling, Christie replied, "I think you're a lot more "okay" than you give yourself credit for."

Frowning, Addy clearly didn't understand.

Leaning forward, Christie told her, "You've got a clear understanding of what you've just been through. You are ready to move on, but have worries, which is very normal, and you've recognized that you have a physical attraction to someone."

Smiling, Adalyn nodded back to her therapist. "He says things that make me calm."

"Really?" Christie asked. "What does he say?"

Thinking about her encounter with Kian earlier in the day, Addy answered, "It's not what he says, but how he says it, that calms me."

Christie asked, "Is Kian the hot, Irish guy I've seen around here?"

At Christie's very non-professional description of Kian, Addy laughed, and nodded. "Yes, he is."

Shrugging, Christie replied, "Well, I think if I got to work with him almost every day, I might feel my stomach tighten up too," and she winked at Adalyn.

"He makes me work hard," Adalyn offered, "and he knows how to rile me up so I work harder."

Smiling, Christie said, "Well, it sounds like he's a great physical therapist then since that's what they're supposed to do."

Adalyn pondered her words for a minute or so, "He was talking to me today, very soft...ly, and I wanted him to kiss me."

Surprised by Adalyn's admission, Christie asked, "Did you tell him how he makes you feel?"

Stunned at the prospect of admitting something like that to Kian, or anyone else, had Adalyn leaning back and shaking her head vehemently, saying, "Oh, no."

"Why not?" Christie asked her.

Picking up the tablet, Adalyn typed... *I was engaged before I got into the accident. He cheated on me. What if Kian doesn't like me? I don't want to feel that rejection.*

Christie considered the words, then responded with, "I wasn't there, I'll admit it, but, from what you've said, I'd say he's at least interested in you."

Changing the subject completely, Adalyn said, "I may get to go home next week."

Knowing that when Adalyn changed the subject, she was done with it, for now at least, Christie spoke to her about going home and what that would entail. She knew that Adalyn couldn't hide her feelings from Kian, but unless she was willing to take the risk and talk to him about it, there would be nothing gained.

When Adalyn returned to her room, she gasped when she saw all the flowers. There were bouquets all around, colorful designs of roses, gardenias, and about thirty other kinds she couldn't name. Looking at her mother, she asked, "Who sent these?"

Irritated still, but not wanting to show Adalyn how much, Evelyn drew a steadying breath before turning around to answer her daughter. "I guess Tommy decided to let your old publicist know about your change in condition, so there was a press release in the papers here in Houston and out in Los Angeles. A lot of these are from your old friends, and fans."

Slowly making her way around the room, Addy read every card. Most of them said things like, "Can't wait to see you," or "When will we see pictures of you?"

Evelyn watched her daughter, hoping that all of this wasn't too much. "I know you've said you don't want to model again, but it looks like they'll take you back if you want."

Shaking her head in denial, Adalyn answered, "No," she looked at her mother, her gaze steady, and added, "I'm not doing that anymore."

Relieved, Evelyn nodded in return. She feared that lifestyle before Addy's accident, and even blamed it to some aspect for causing the accident and subsequent coma. If it weren't for her modeling, she'd never have met Tommy and then she'd never have caught him in bed with Jeni only days before their wedding. Just thinking about it all made Evelyn's blood boil. They'd tried to be open with Addy about the circumstances surrounding the accident, but it still hurt both her and Doug. They would do whatever they had to in order to protect Addy. And if that meant, keeping the vultures from her past life at bay, then that's what they would do. "Good," She said to Addy, "we'll be sure to release that as well."

As Addy got ready for bed, with her mother still hovering, she smiled, and said, "Mom, it will be okay, I'm stro....nger than I look."

Evelyn hugged her daughter, "Oh, sweetie, your dad and I know that."

"Good," Addy replied.

Chapter 11

Adalyn worked very hard during the next week. She resigned herself to getting out of the hospital, no matter what it would mean for her, emotionally. She needed to step out and start living again. She'd had three calls from her agent and finally spoke to her, saying that she was no longer interested in doing modeling. All the morning talk shows wanted her to appear, and she was getting calls from a variety of magazines, who wanted to do her "story."

As far as Adalyn was concerned, her story wasn't all that exciting. And she didn't want to tell the world about it, even if they thought it was. If there was one thing she learned from modeling all those years, it was that fame was fleeting, and the only thing that counted was that you worked hard and kept your word.

By Thursday, her nerves were shot. The sound of Kian coming into the room actually startled her out of her thoughts.

"What's wrong?" Kian asked, a serious tone lacing his words.

Shaking her head, Adalyn simply answered, "Nothing."

Kian put down his bag, and asked her, "Do ya think I'm a spanner?"

Having no idea what a "spanner" was, Adalyn smiled, and responded with a tentative, "No."

"Good," He said, "cause it's not in the least bit flatterin.'"

His words and tone made her smile widen. "How do you do that?" She asked him bluntly.

Walking over to where she stood, near the window, Kian asked her, "Do what?"

Adalyn turned so she was facing him fully. "How do you know how to make me laugh?"

Kian nodded, as if he knew something. "Easy," He answered, "we Irish have the hearts of poets, the tongues of lovers, and the wit of the.......wittiest."

Now his nonsensical words made her laugh outright.

"There's the pretty lass, I know," Kian said, his eyes darkening with awareness.

She looked down at her feet, for a moment, and then back up to him, before asking, "Do you think I'm pretty?"

Reaching out, Kian snatched Adalyn's hand, and put it into his own, before responding with, "Oh, there's no one prettier than the feek who stands before me."

Her eyes widening, Adalyn said, "I'm not sure whether to feel com...plimen...ted or in...sul...ted."

Squeezing her hand lightly, Kian brought it up and kissed the back of it. "A feek is a gorgeous woman."

"Well, I'd suggest you Irish find a better sounding word for that then," Adalyn winked at him.

Now it was Kian's turn to laugh. "I'll try to find ya anudder word that sounds sweeter," he emphasized his Irish accent.

Even though Adalyn liked the way her hand felt, tucked into his, she knew they had to get to work. "Okay, enough with you, you Irish rogue, let's get to work."

His eyebrows raised, Kian answered, "Okay," he added, "Although I thought I was the one to be handing out the orders here."

Giving him a bland look, Adalyn retorted, "Kian, you are a man, you are never the one giving out orders."

He laughed, and said, "I believe you would be right to say so."

They walked over to where his bag sat, the awkward moments done with, for now.

Later that evening, Nurse Suzie and Nurse Janice came in with a little cake. It had one single candle in it. Suzie smiled as they walked into Adalyn's room. "I had a friend of mine make this for you, it's sooooo good!"

Adalyn dutifully blew out the candle, to the applause of the nurses, and then took a bite. "Oh," She said, her eyes wide, "this is really good."

The two nurses sat down for a few minutes and actually visited with Adalyn. They talked about Suzie's friend, who made the cake, and how Suzie was trying to get her to start up an actual business. Janice showed Adalyn pictures of her three kids and it was so nice just to talk, without focusing on what Addy had been through, or what she needed to do in order to get back to "normal."

After this experience, Adalyn had grown very irritated with the word "normal" and felt it had no place in her life anymore. Normal wasn't comparing yourself to the masses; normal was what you chose to spend your own life doing and not giving one whit as to what others thought of you.

The nurses left soon after, and Adalyn drifted off into the best sleep she'd had in over a week. It was a dream filled with possibilities, rather than one with limitations or fears.

Kian came home Friday, and was exhausted. He'd been putting in extra hours with Adalyn, to get her ready for the transition to home life, so, by the time he got home, he was wiped out. Tonight, he happened to run into his neighbor, Missy, "Uh, hi," he said to her, surprised to see her this late.

"Hi, Kian," Missy returned, wringing her hands. "I was wondering if you were available for that dinner tonight."

He really wanted to say yes, but, the truth was, he was beat. "I don't mean to disappoint ya, but I'm just too tired to be of good company this particular evening."

Missy nodded, but she couldn't hide the disappointment in her expression. "It's okay," She said to him, and went up to her apartment.

Kian watched her walk away, rejection reflected in the way she held her shoulders. "Wait up, Missy," He shouted, and jogged over to her. "Just give me a few minutes to get myself in order, and we'll go get some dinner."

Smiling wide, Missy shook her head, "I actually made dinner at my apartment, so you wouldn't have to bother with all of that."

His neighbor was a gem, Kian knew it now. "Oh, that would be grand. I'll just clean up and pop over in a few."

"Okay," Missy said, and started walking again.

Kian ran up to his apartment, and showered, and dressed in record time. It was so nice of her to make dinner at her apartment. He was at her door in about fifteen minutes, a bottle of wine in his hands. "My ma told me, you never go to a house for dinner without bringing something as a gift," He handed her the bottle.

"Thank you," Missy answered shyly. She motioned for him to sit in the living room. "Dinner will be ready in about five minutes, I'm just putting the finishing touches on it."

Kian walked into her living room, a mirror of his own in size, and sat down. Her furniture was small, but comfortable looking. Her apartment was neat and tidy, much like the woman herself appeared to be.

Missy walked out of the kitchen a few minutes later, two glasses of wine in her hands. She handed one to Kian, then sat down in the chair adjacent to the sofa he was seated on. "So," She started, "I know that we don't know much about one another, even though we've lived in the same building for two years now."

Nodding, Kian leaned forward, and sipped his wine. "I'd say that's the gist of it all," He prodded her to continue.

After taking a generous gulp of her wine, Missy explained that she was a dental hygienist, and worked in Pearland.

There was a timer that went off, and she hurried off to the kitchen. Kian sat there, and thought, even though she was a lovely person, he had absolutely no interest in getting to know her. Visions of Adalyn Phillips filled his mind and spun around his head constantly.

"Dinner is ready," Missy announced from the kitchen, so Kian grabbed their glasses of wine and went into the dining room area.

His eyes widened in surprise. The woman must cook like a fiend, the table was done finer than any five star restaurant he'd ever been too. "My, oh my, Missy," Kian said, "Ya didn't have to be goin to all dis trouble for dinner."

Wringing her hands once again, she responded, "Oh, I wanted to impress you."

They sat down, and ate. Kian praised her efforts and couldn't remember when he'd had a finer meal. After his second helping of the roast, potatoes, and carrots, he sat back. "Oh my, I'll be rolling myself home, I'm so stuffed with the wonderful food ya made."

Blushing, Missy started to get up and collect the dishes, "I'm so glad you enjoyed it," she said.

"I did, indeed," Kian replied, and stood to help her clear the table. When she tried to tell him he didn't have to help, he told her that his mother would wring his neck if he didn't help out a lady who'd made such a fine meal.

They stood, side-by-side, and rinsed dishes, with Missy loading them into the dishwasher.

Kian knew this was something he could get used to, but, again, thoughts of Adalyn filled his mind.

"She's a lucky woman," Missy commented, and smiled at Kian's look of shame.

Trying to salvage his manners, Kian asked, "Why do you say that?"

Missy dried her hands with the dish towel, and neatly folded it over the designated place in her kitchen. "Kian, I'm a woman who's quiet, and orderly, and plain." She sighed, "It took me two years to get up the courage to ask you out," she tipped her head to study him, "but I'm not blind, and I only wish you'd wear that look when you thought of me."

Oh, this woman was a doll! Kian stepped forward and kissed her forehead, "Yer are a grand lady, I'll tell you that, and, I swear, if my heart wasn't already snatched up, I'd be in love with ya the minute I tasted yer food."

Giggling, partly because she was covering her disappointment at being right, and partly because of his close proximity. "There will be a nice CPA or lawyer who will come along and find me irresistible, right?" She asked him.

Kian nodded, "Oh yes, and he'd better be right by you or he'll be havin me to contend with."

Walking him to the door, Missy leaned over and kissed Kian's cheek, "Thank you."

"It's me who should be thankin you alright," He winked, "of course I'll not have to eat for some days now, you've fattened me up right good."

Missy opened the door, and shook her head endearingly, "I doubt that."

As Kian walked back to his apartment, he thought about the lovely Missy, and hoped only the best for her. Then his thoughts turned to Adalyn, and the fever of love ran through his veins. Oh, that one, she'll be the woman who sets him aflame for the rest of his life. He smiled, remembering that his father said those exact words about his mother, and he never understood them, until this moment. "Oh, Adalyn Phillips, may the good Lord love ya, and may he let you love me."

Addy knew that her time here at the rehabilitation center, was nearing the end. She was due to meet up with her medical team once again. This time, it was to plan out what care she would continue with, once she left the center.

The same players were present, the doctors who managed her speech, Kian, his boss, Sheri, Dr. Gruen, Dr. Cooper, her parents, and now, Christie joined them.

"So," Dr. Cooper started, once everyone was seated, "I don't think any of us could've thought we'd be sitting here, planning your homecoming, Adalyn."

Kian pretended to look at his notebook, instead of glaring at the smooth talking doctor.

Dr. Cooper nodded toward Dr. Tillman, and asked, "So, what are your recommendations?"

Handing out copies of a report, Dr. Tillman described the schedule that Adalyn had been doing since she woke up, and that his recommendation was that she continue physical therapy at home, with Kian going there to do her sessions.

Looking at the Phillips family, Dr. Cooper asked them, "Are you all on board with that?"

Evelyn and Doug nodded, and Adalyn answered, "Yes."

Next, the speech pathologist and therapist talked about what they planned for Adalyn.

Christie was the last one to speak, suggesting that Adalyn continue her therapy sessions for at least another couple of months, to help her adjust to her life once again.

The plan was a solid one, with everyone in agreement, so the meeting didn't even take an hour.

Adalyn sat there, and felt as if they were discussing someone else besides her. This felt like some movie where an alternate universe existed, and she was caught up in it. Before they all left, she stood up and said, "I want to thank every single one of you." She looked around the table, "None of you gave up on me, and I appreciate that."

Dr. Cooper looked at her, and said, "Adalyn, it was you who never gave up."

There were some "Here, here's," and someone said "Amen," and everyone clapped.

Evelyn guided her daughter out of the room, and kissed her cheek. "Are you excited to go home?" She asked Addy.

"Yes and no," Addy answered. "I'm glad that I'll be in a real room, with a real bed," she sighed, "but I'm also scared."

Smiling at her daughter, Evelyn said, "Welcome to life."

Chapter 12

Adalyn spent her last night at the rehabilitation center, talking to other patients, the nurses, the doctors, and the volunteers. Everyone wished her well and asked that she keep them posted on her progress. In some ways, it felt like she was being freed from a prison, and, in others, it was like she was being turned out into the cold.

The next morning, bright and early, her parents arrived to pick her up.

She'd just come out of the bathroom, in her robe, and saw their smiling faces. "Good morning," She said.

Evelyn smiled, "Good morning," she returned, then asked, "Are you ready?"

Adalyn sighed, and answered, "I'm as ready as I'll ever be, I suppose."

Doug handed her a garment bag. "Mom brought one of your outfits," He said, and smiled.

Taking the bag, Addy went back into the bathroom. She hung the bag up on the back of the door and unzipped it. Inside was a gorgeous dress in a salmon color. The fabric was flimsy, and Adalyn could see it paired with a colorful scarf and flirty sandals. Shaking her head, she said to herself, "It's not all about how you look anymore," and took the dress out of the bag.

Half an hour later, she emerged from the bathroom. Her hair was long now, as her parents didn't have it cut during her time in the coma, and she just brushed it until it shone in soft waves halfway down her back.

Doug and Evelyn watched their daughter walk out of the bathroom, then they looked at one another, and smiled.

Walking over to her daughter, Evelyn hugged Addy, and commented, "You look breathtaking."

Adalyn stood there, smiling at her mother, and thinking just the opposite. After she dressed, she took a long look in the bathroom mirror. Her hair was longer, yes, but it wasn't healthy looking, her limbs were still scrawny, and she still felt tired. Understanding that, to her mother, she probably appeared breathtaking because only weeks earlier, she'd been a vegetable, she replied, "Thanks, Mom."

They packed up what few things Adalyn wanted to take with her, and were about to leave when they were met by Dr. Cooper.

"All set?" Dr. Cooper asked the Phillips'.

Nodding, Adalyn replied, "I guess."

He could understand Adalyn's reluctance. This constant barrage of change in her life was exhausting for her. He couldn't begin to think what missing three years of her life was doing to her emotionally; although Christie reported to him that she was handling the acclimation to her life better than they all expected. Looking at Adalyn Phillips, in her pretty dress, he imagined that she was no stranger to surprising people. He stepped forward and shook her hand, saying, "I'll see you next week for your appointment and you can tell me all about the food outside this place."

The joke wasn't lost on Addy, and she smiled. "I'm hopeful that my mom's cooking has stayed as great as it used to be."

Evelyn rolled her eyes, and Doug laughed.

"Good luck," Dr. Cooper said, then handed Doug Phillips a clipboard with papers on it, and asked him, "Could you please sign these for Adalyn's discharge?"

Adalyn and Evelyn started out of the room and into the hallway as Doug finished up with Dr. Cooper. The nurses waved to them as they left.

As if on cue, the sun started peeking through the clouds as they came out of the rehabilitation center. It was as if she was coming out of the clouds in her life, and into the sunlight. They were making their way to the car when Adalyn saw Kian getting out of his car. She stopped, and waited.

Seeing Kian, Evelyn realized that her daughter wanted to speak to him, so she whispered, "I'll just go start up the car and put your bag inside."

Nodding to her mother, Addy stood there, not moving. She knew it the moment Kian spotted her because he paused mid-step. It wasn't for but a second or two, but Addy noticed, and his reaction made her smile.

Kian was coming into work when he saw Adalyn standing on the sidewalk, outside of the center. Oh, his heart was beatin like thunder in his chest. She was a vision, if he ever knew one. Walking toward her, he could see a bit of nervousness in how she held herself. "Saints preserve us," He exclaimed, and smiled brightly at her as he came closer, "You are a vision of beauty."

The compliment was just what Addy needed to shore up her confidence. "Thank you," She answered, and was so happy that her mother brought the pretty dress for her to wear.

"So, what are yer big plans, now that yer free from this place?" He asked as he pointed to the center.

Shrugging, Adalyn replied, "Not sure yet, but," she smiled, "don't forget that we have our standing therapy appointments."

As if he could forget, Kian thought to himself. "I've not forgotten and yer father gave me your new address, and I'll be there."

She couldn't tell him that his time with her was the bright spot in her, otherwise stressful day, so she just kept smiling. When her father came up behind her, she raised her hand in a quick wave, and said, "Okay, bye then," to Kian.

As he watched Adalyn leave with her parents, Kian felt an emotional tearing in his chest. He would still continue with her physical therapy, but it wasn't going to be daily now. He stood on the sidewalk, and watched Adalyn and her parents drive away before walking inside to meet up with Mrs. Wilkins.

Twenty minutes later, Kian was already frustrated. Mostly due to the fact that all Mrs. Wilkins wanted to talk about, was Adalyn Phillips. How they chatted the day before about all sorts of things, how Adalyn reminded her of her daughter, and how it was just such a miracle that the young woman came out of the coma.

They were working on Mrs. Wilkins' balance when Kian found himself actually scowling at the woman. Shaking himself mentally, he pasted his usual smile on, and got back down to business. His personal feelings on the subject of one Miss Adalyn Phillips needed to be put on hold for the time being.

Adalyn peered out the car window as her parents drove down Hwy 35 South toward Alvin, Texas. They had just bought the house; they called their retirement home, a week before Addy's accident, so she'd never even seen it. When she was moved to a long-term facility, they requested she be placed in one closer to them and she was glad they'd done that. If she was still in the hospital closer to Dallas, it would have been very inconvenient for them.

Over the last couple of days, she had been prodding information from her parents about what happened right after her accident. Even though she could see how hard it was for them, her mother tried to be as open and honest as she could.

After the accident, she stayed in ICU for two weeks. Finding out that Tommy actually requested she be taken off of life support was a nasty blow, but she realized that was what upset her parents so much about seeing him. He was willing to just throw her away, because he felt nothing for her. Taking her money was something they could all get over, but wanting to actually end her life was pretty unforgiveable.

"We're almost there," Evelyn said over her shoulder.

Adalyn nodded, and kept looking out the window. It was late spring now; the brown spots on the ground, from the winter, were almost faded, such as it was here in Texas. The trees were full of buds or new leaves, so that meant that spring was definitely here.

Her father pulled the car off onto a county road, and drove a few more minutes before he pulled into a driveway. The house was white, with dark red shutters around the windows. There was a red front door, with an oval piece of glass in the center, etched with a flower design.

Evelyn said, "It's not like our other house," to her daughter.

Addy realized it wasn't like the childhood home her parents had before. It was adorable though, and she couldn't wait to get inside and explore it.

Before her dad could even get out of the driver's side, Adalyn was pushing her door open and getting out. She held on to the door a moment longer than most people would, just to get her bearings and her equilibrium. Sometimes, when she stood up too fast, she felt off kilter. Her mother got out, and offered Addy her hand.

They were entering in the back door, and had to get up three stairs. Even though Kian had worked with her, Adalyn found the stairs a difficult obstacle. She leaned against her parents, who were on either side of her now, as they went up.

"It's adorable," Adalyn whispered as her father unlocked the door.

Evelyn smiled. "That's exactly what I told your dad when we first looked at it."

Nodding, Doug mumbled, "Sure, until she gave me the honey-do-list that came along with it."

Adalyn chuckled. It was good to see her parents joke with one another, and her. It provided a sense of normalcy, and that was something Adalyn craved.

Once inside, there was a small foyer, complete with a bench and coatrack done up in a dark wood. It was flanked on either side by large light sconces. Adalyn looked both ways, seeing a kitchen on her left, and the dining table to her right. "Which way?" She asked her mother.

Evelyn led her daughter to the left, and into the compact, but neatly laid out kitchen. It had a retro look to it, with subway tiles as a back splash and an island in the middle, which had to stove in it. There were 3 small benches set underneath the island overhang. On the far side of the room was a breakfast nook that was all windows on one side. Addy gravitated straight for it, smiling as she looked outside.

"I knew you'd love it," Evelyn said, as she came up behind her daughter. "I pictured us having coffee in the mornings when you visited."

There was a small, round table with four chairs in the space and the pale yellow wall, across from the windows made the room look cheerful and welcoming.

Doug led them through a different small, hallway with a bathroom on the left, that he explained would be the one Adalyn would use, and a closet on the right for the washer and dryer.

After passing through the small hallway, they came into the main living space. It spanned the entire width of the house, with the living room on one end and the dining table at the other. Her mother took great pains with the color schemes and accent pieces so it looked like something out of magazine. "It's so cozy," Adalyn said to her mother, and gained a smile for it.

They went down another hallway that had two doors at the far end, one on each side. "This," Her mother pointed to the room on the right, "is yours."

Entering the room, Adalyn smiled widely. The walls were done in a pale rose color. There was an accent shelf about a foot below the ceiling, and was just wide enough to hold little knick knacks on it. There was a bed against one wall, opposite from the window, and had a white, iron headboard and footboard. The comforter was a very pale pink and the accent pillows were all shades of pink with flower patterns. There were two white night stands that flanked the bed, and a large dresser on one wall with a large, white armoire on the other.

"The closet isn't very big," Doug told his daughter, "so we had that piece put in."

Adalyn stood in the room that would be hers, and started to cry.

Doug and Evelyn gave one another a startled look, before going over and hugging their daughter.

Evelyn asked her, "Are you okay? Do you hate it?"

Smiling through the tears, Addy pulled back and told her mother, "No, I'm crying because it's just so beautiful."

Relieved, Doug patted his daughter on the back, then left the room.

"Did I upset him?" Adalyn asked her mother, after her father left.

Evelyn shook her head, "No," she answered, "He's just like I am," she sat down on the bed, and patted the space beside her for her daughter to join her. "We're both so happy and so scared at the same time."

Adalyn sat down, and hugged her mother again. "I am too."

Just having her baby here was a Blessing that she could have never considered, and Evelyn wasn't about to not be grateful for it. "I guess this is one of those life lessons that I can't really "teach" you, we'll both have to learn it together."

Smiling, Addy said, "And I'm so happy that I have you and Dad to learn it with."

Chapter 13

The next two days were more difficult than Addy thought they would be. The most notable difference was the quiet. Her parents bought a house on a large lot, with very quiet neighbors. At night, when she was used to being checked in on by nurses, and hearing the sounds of machines and other people, she only heard silence, or the chirping of the crickets outside. It was unnerving on a lot of levels.

On the third day, Kian was slated to come to the house for her physical therapy session. For some reason, that morning Addy woke up with a lighter feeling inside. She walked into the kitchen and, without thinking, went over to the coffee maker, poured herself a cup, and went into the breakfast nook to join her parents. She'd just taken the first sip, after sitting down, when she noticed her parents staring at her. "What's wrong?" She asked them, worried about the way they were looking at her.

Evelyn spoke first, "Uh, nothing……except that you don't, or didn't I mean, drink coffee."

Taking another sip, Addy thought the feel of the warm liquid felt good. She was starting to wake up now. "You know," She said to her parents, "I didn't even think about it, I just did it."

Doug watched his daughter, and smiled, "Well, at least we know you like coffee now."

The three of them laughed it off, and wondered what other changes they would discover in Adalyn.

Kian followed his GPS and thought the drive to the Phillips' house was nice. He normally stayed in Pearland, since it was a booming area and had everything he needed. Down here, near Alvin, was more peaceful, and not as far from the "city" as he thought. When he pulled into the driveway, he was surprised to see Adalyn sitting outside, on the back porch, and seemingly waiting for him. After getting out, he hollered over the top of the car, "Well, aren't you a fine sight on this beautiful mornin."

Adalyn blushed, and returned, "Aren't you a sight for sore eyes."

Smiling back at her, Kian went to the trunk to retrieve his bags. He decided they no longer needed the portable table he had since Adalyn was, for all intent and purposes, completely mobile now. After getting his things, he shut the trunk, and started toward the house. "Are you ready to work?" He asked her as he started up the stairs.

Standing up, Addy nodded, "Yes sir," she answered and led the way inside.

They walked into the kitchen, and were greeted by Mr. and Mrs. Phillips. Evelyn stood, and asked, "Can I get you something to drink, Kian?"

Kian shook his head no, and answered, "I appreciate da offer Mr. Phillips, but it's time to be gettin down to work."

Evelyn recognized the professional tone, and wondered if something had transpired between Addy and the young man that she didn't know about. "Okay," She replied, "We're going outside to do some lawn work, just yell out the back door if you need anything." She motioned for a grumbling Doug to follow her.

Adalyn watched her parents go out the back door, her father clearly not happy about the prospect of yard work, and smiled. "I think they wanted to give us privacy." She turned to motion for Kian to follow her.

They walked down the short hallway, through the great room, down the longer hallway ahead, and ended up on the enclosed porch at the front of the house.

"This is lovely," Kian commented as he put his bag down, unzipped it, and began rummaging through it for the needed resistance bands they would be using during this session.

Earlier, while Addy was getting ready, she'd come out to the porch, and opened all the blinds. It was a little too humid out to open the windows, but she wanted to feel the sunlight pour into the room as they worked. It lifted her spirits and, according to Christie, her therapist, she needed to stick with things that lifted her spirits until she was adjusted to her surroundings again.

"So," Kian said, as he motioned for Adalyn to sit on the yoga mat he'd put on the floor, "How is it being out of the rehabilitation center?"

Adalyn rolled her eyes, not because she was irritated with Kian, but because it was the one question that everyone she'd spoken to, over the last couple of days, felt compelled to ask her. "It's fine."

Sitting down beside her, Kian silently started to help her with some stretching exercises. After a few minutes, he said, "Your tone is sayin you're plain tired of hearin it."

Feeling like a jerk, she looked over at Kian, and responded, "I'm sorry, everyone keeps asking me that," she said, and then added, "It's fine, just really quiet here."

Kian continued with helping her stretch out, only nodding in acknowledgement. He felt it was better to be a little less invasive with his questions for the time being.

They got through the required leg exercises, and were working on the arm exercises, when Kian asked her, "What have ya been doin for some fun then?"

"Fun?" Adalyn responded in surprise. "Uh," She said, flustered, "I'm not sure what you mean."

Sitting back, surprised himself, Kian asked, "Do ya not know the meanin of the word fun, lass?"

His accent, combined with the question, made Adalyn laugh. "I do," She said a little defensively. "But," She said as she lifted the 2 lb. weight up with her right hand, "It's not like people are at the door or calling to invite me out."

"Why do ya suppose that is?" Kian asked, making conversation as they worked through the set.

Adalyn stopped doing the bicep curl, and looked at him, before answering, "I think, honestly, it's because they all think I might up and die, or slip back into the coma, or God knows what else."

Her reply made Kian take notice. Here he was, thinking that all the attention on her was that of acceptance, when it was really of distance. People were afraid for some reason, although he was clueless as to why. Perhaps he wasn't afraid because he'd been working with her during this whole process. "I think ya need to get out." He said, with conviction.

Feeling snippy, Adalyn came back with, "Are you going to be the one to take me?" She realized, as soon as the words left her mouth, that they were practically a dare.

Two things occurred to Kian, as they sat there, neither moving, on the floor of the porch. The first thing was, that she didn't stutter in the least bit, especially when she was angry. She was developing quite a backbone, and he was glad to hear it. The second thing was, that she seemed lonely, even being here with her parents. He retorted, "Well, yes, I'll be happy to take ya out to wherever you want to go."

Great! Addy thought to herself, now he's just taking pity on me. "I don't need your pity date," She mumbled.

Feeling his own anger take a turn, Kian stopped what he was doing, and turned to cup her face in his palms. "Now, ya don't need to be a brat about this, Adalyn, I was offerin because I tink of ya as a friend."

Again, she felt bad. "I'm sorry," She replied, and sat there, staring at him intently. He was serious, she could see that. After about a minute, he released his hold on her face, and picked up a weight out of his bag.

Addy took the weight he was holding to start her next set of arm exercises. "I know you are only trying to be nice." She did the required triceps curl, and then said, "I never know what anyone wants from me anymore."

Reaching up, Kian stopped her from continuing the set. "Well, I'll tell ya that yer parents only want ya to be happy, and that's what I'm hopin for too." He waited for her to nod, then said, "It's easy for the rest of us to pass judgment on ya, because we don't know what you've been through."

The rational side of her mind knew he was only speaking the truth, but it didn't stop her heart from beating funny because of the way his eyes looked at her. There was something more intense about them right now. And now that they were away from the rehab center, that feeling of "awareness" was constant. "I'm trying to deal with it the best way I can."

Forgetting himself, Kian ran the back of his hand gently along Addy's cheek. It was an intimate move, one he knew he shouldn't do, and yet, he felt helpless to stop it. Being with her before, was difficult enough. Now, they were practically alone, and he couldn't help the raging emotions that flooded through him at the sight of her.

"Why did you do that?" Adalyn asked him, point blank.

Sighing, Kian answered, "Because, Mo Milis, ya need to be taken care of and shown compassion."

Her insides took a leap, as if they were trying to find their footing, and Adalyn sighed. "What does that mean, mo milis?" She asked Kian.

Putting the weight, in her other hand, Kian tried to fight off his feelings, and replied, "Ya get yourself better, and I'll tell ya."

An hour later, Kian was pulling out of the driveway, and Adalyn stood on the porch, watching him drive away, with her mother by her side.

"How did it go?" Evelyn asked her daughter.

Looking over, Addy answered, "The physical therapy was okay, it's getting a little easier, but there is something about him that makes my insides uneasy."

"Uneasy?" Evelyn asked, fear for her daughter popping up inside her chest.

Adalyn shook her head, "Not in a bad way," she turned to walk inside, "in a weird way."

Not having had this kind of talk with her daughter before, Evelyn was not sure how to start. She dove into the subject with, "Do you have feelings for him?"

Adalyn shut the door behind them, and followed her mother into the kitchen. She sat down on a bar stool as her mother pulled out the fixings for their lunch. She watched her mom for a few minutes, before answering, "I think so," then followed with, "but after making that horrific mistake with Tommy, I wonder if I can trust myself."

Evelyn nodded as her daughter spoke. She didn't look up, because she didn't want Addy to see how the words affected her. There was still so much residual anger and frustration with the situation involving her daughter's relationship with Tommy and Jeni. "I think," She started, finally looking up, "that you can probably trust yourself much more now, than you could then."

Addy was surprised and furrowed her brow.

"Now," Evelyn explained, "you have the experience of what you don't want, i.e, Tommy." She kept cutting the lettuce they would use for their lunch salad, "Now you can work with what your instincts are telling you."

Her mother's words made sense. "Maybe I should ask Christie about it," Addy said, "she said that sometimes patients develop dependent relationships with their caregivers."

Evelyn nodded, and said, "I can understand that," then continued, "But I don't really see that with you and Kian." She put the cut up lettuce into a large bowl, and asked Addy, "You don't rely on him to get you through your day, do you?"

Addy shook her head, and answered, "No."

"That's a good thing," Evelyn stated, and smiled as her husband walked in through the back door, a frown on his face from having to do yard work. "We'll continue this talk later," She said as she nodded toward Doug.

Adalyn giggled, and nodded in reply.

That evening, Addy was on Facebook, scrolling through her mother's account, laughing at the crazy pictures some people posted, and appalled at some of the other things people were willing to say on a public site. Her mother went through with her how to log in, and suggested she make her own page. There was one, years ago, for her modeling, but that was discontinued when she went into the coma, and the doctors predicted she wouldn't come out.

She was still scrolling when a little box popped up in the bottom, right corner of her screen. It was labeled from Kian Fitzpatrick, and the message read.....*Mrs. Phillips, I'm sorry I didn't get a chance to speak to you and Mr. Phillips today after Adalyn's session. She is doing very well and is exceeding our expectations in her recovery.*

The professionalism of his message had Adalyn cringing. She decided to answer for her mother and typed....*Thank you for letting us know. We know Addy really enjoys working with you. She said you offered to take her out today.*

Addy watched the little label say that the message was read, and eagerly watched the little bubble that popped up saying that he was replying. She smiled when she saw the words.......*I did. I think that Adalyn is very unsure of her social skills, and being a friend, I wanted to help.*

Help, schmelp, she thought to herself. There was no way that she could think that he didn't feel what she felt. If he didn't, then Addy really wouldn't be able to trust herself, and that wasn't what her mother said, and what she believed. Typing back, she said......*I'm afraid Adalyn may view this as more than a "friend" type situation. Does that concern you?*

Might as well put it all out there, Adalyn said to herself. She was waiting for the response when her dad came up behind her, and asked, "Anything good?"

Before she could see what Kian replied, she shut down the page and turned to him, smiling, "Nope." She stood, kissed her dad on the cheek, and announced, "I'm going to go and get ready for bed." And left the room as quickly as she could.

An hour later, Evelyn popped onto Facebook to see what was going on, when she noticed she had a message. Opening it up, she read.....*I might as well be honest with you and Mr. Phillips, I've had feelings for Adalyn for some time now. I don't want to scare you into thinking that it's a stalker kind of situation or anything, but I shouldn't be afraid to let you both know.*

Evelyn, intrigued, went back to read the conversation. Clearly, Addy was acting as her and wheedling out information from Kian. She admired her daughter for her tenacity, but was a little concerned that she was hiding behind her mother in order to get it. Logging off, she decided to go and talk to her husband about what she read.

Chapter 14

Two days later, Kian returned for their session. He'd been going over the facebook conversation with Adalyn's mother in his mind, and still didn't have any answers. She hadn't responded after his last message about having feelings for Adalyn.

After parking in the driveway, he went up and knocked on the back door. Mr. Phillips appeared through the glass, smiling, which Kian took as a good sign.

"Kian, come in," Doug said as he opened the door. "How are you today?"

Smiling in return, Kian entered the house, and answered, "Fine as the mornin rain on a clear day in Ireland."

Not understanding why the morning rain was fine, Doug simply nodded, and said, "Good."

They walked into the dining room, where Evelyn and Adalyn were sitting at the table, and going through picture albums.

"Good morning, Kian," Evelyn said as she looked up from her task.

Kian nodded to Mrs. Phillips, and replied, "A good mornin to you as well."

The three of them watched, as Adalyn continued to look at the picture album, seemingly unaware that they were even in the room.

"Addy," Doug said, and glanced at his wife, when his daughter didn't respond.

Getting worried, Evelyn reached over and touched Addy's arm, saying, "Adalyn," but getting no answer.

Kian dropped his bag and crossed over to where Adalyn was very still. He grabbed a flashlight out of his pants pocket, and flashed the light in Adalyn's eyes. All of a sudden, she popped out of whatever trance she was in.

"What?" Adalyn asked, and noticed that Kian was right in front of her, only inches from her face. "Kian, what are you doing?" She asked him, embarrassed.

Trying to remain calm, Kian stepped back from Adalyn and turned to her parents, saying, "I'd like you to call Dr. Cooper and explain that Adalyn has just had a possible seizure."

All Evelyn heard was seizure, and she started to panic. Looking over at her husband, who was giving her the "don't fall apart," look, she nodded and went to grab her cell phone in the kitchen.

Adalyn watched her parents leave the room, and looked pointedly at Kian, "What are you talking about?" She asked him.

Sitting down next to her, Kian answered, "Your parents were talking to you, and you didn't respond."

Blowing it off, and feeling irritated, she retorted, "You're all just being paranoid."

Getting ticked off himself, Kian snapped back, "Don't ya take yer health for granted!" He stood up and started pacing a few feet away, "Yer dear parents are worried sick, and ya have the nerve to get on acting the maggot."

Not understanding what Kian was saying, Addy stared at him. It wasn't difficult though, given his tone, to what he was referring. She dropped her hands into her lap, and said, "I'm sorry."

Doug and Evelyn came back into the room. The atmosphere was thick with tension, and everyone could feel it. If she weren't so busy worrying about her daughter, Evelyn would have asked what happened. Instead she announced, "Dr. Cooper wants to see us, now."

Adalyn nodded to her mother, and stood up, feeling woozy for just a few seconds, she swayed.

Kian saw Adalyn was off-balance and shot over to help her find her balance. She grabbed onto him, and held on, all the while, just being silent.

"Let's go," Doug said, and they all four left the house.

An hour later, they were at the rehabilitation center, and Adalyn was hooked up to an EEG machine, to measure her brain activity.

Doug, Evelyn, and Kian waited out in the hallway, per Dr. Cooper's instructions. He wanted to talk to Adalyn about what she experienced and didn't want her answers to be influenced by what her parents, or Kian, experienced.

A few minutes later, Dr. Cooper emerged from the room, smiling. "She's getting dressed," He told the three of them. "I think it was just an absence seizure, and we didn't notice them while she was here." They started walking down the hall toward his office, "I've called one of my colleagues to consult, but I think it was a fluke." He motioned for all of them to sit down. "We have to remember that she had a traumatic brain injury, and we don't know what kind of coping mechanisms her brain will come up with." He looked at the Phillips' and asked, "What was she doing right before you noticed her zoning out?"

Evelyn answered, "She and I were looking through photo albums from when she was a child."

Then Doug spoke up, saying, "I had just answered the door to Kian, and we were walking into the dining room so she could start her physical therapy."

"I'm not going to go into another coma, am I?" They all turned around at the sound of Adalyn's question.

Dr. Cooper stood, and motioned for Adalyn to come in and have a seat, before answering, "We don't think so."

Even though he was saying what she wanted to hear, Addy was pretty sure that he wasn't as positive as he tried to act. "I'm not going back to sleep!" She said vehemently.

Kian reached over and took her hand, "No one said you would."

Snatching her hand back from his, Adalyn stood up, "You're not saying it, but I see people who are unsure." She started to leave the room, "I'm going home," she almost yelled, before walking out into the corridor.

Evelyn stood up first, and raced after her daughter, followed closely by her husband. When Dr. Cooper saw Kian stand up, he said, "It's not like I don't see what's going on."

His head snapping around, Kian knew what the doctor was saying, but didn't want to be judged, not now.

Sensing that Kian was putting up emotional barriers, Dr. Cooper raised his hands in front of him in a gesture of being non-threatening. "I'm not here to judge you," He said to Kian. "I'm just hoping that you know what you're doing."

Stopping halfway to the door, Kian turned around, and asked, "Dr. Cooper, do you know one single person who was thinking rationally and knew what they were doing when they fell in love?"

Smiling, Dr. Cooper simply answered, "Point taken," before watching Kian leave the room.

The ride back to the house was silent.

Kian may have been sitting less than a foot away from Adalyn, but, emotionally, she was halfway round the world. Her mother kept looking back, worriedly, and he tried to smile in order to reassure her. Adalyn just looked out the window.

When Doug pulled into the driveway, he stopped short of the garage so the others could get out before he pulled into the garage. Adalyn got out, slammed the door to the car, and walked up the stairs to the door.

Watching her, Kian couldn't help but admire her. Even in anger, she was determined. Her mother joined her, and unlocked the door. He decided to hold back, and wait for Mr. Phillips, before entering the house.

"Chicken, right?" Doug asked Kian, as he met him in the driveway.

Smiling at Mr. Phillips, Kian answered, "Yer wise cautious in war zones, and when women are mad."

Chuckling, Doug nodded, and responded with, "Good advice."

Kian followed Mr. Phillips into the house. He didn't see Adalyn right away so he followed her father into the kitchen. Mrs. Phillips was putting a kettle on the stove. She looked up when the men entered, and said, "She's on the porch, waiting for you," she pointed to Kian, "and she says she doesn't want her schedule to change."

Doug turned to Kian, "Do you still have time today?"

Luckily, it was a light day for Kian, as far as appointments went. "I'm fine for a bit," He responded, and left the kitchen to meet Adalyn out on the porch.

She was already down on the floor, and stretching out on the yoga mat her mother gave her yesterday. When Kian stepped out onto the porch, she looked up briefly, and nodded in acknowledgement, but didn't say anything.

Kian put down his bag, and grabbed the resistance bands and weights they would be using for this session. He didn't say anything to her, instead he wanted to wait to see what, if anything, Adalyn said to him.

They got to work, first with using the resistance bands to improve Addy's flexibility and toning up her leg muscles.

After the first two sets were completed, Addy could feel the beads of sweat break out on her forehead. It wasn't usually this difficult, but she knew that her emotions were a stumbling block, and causing her physical limitations today.

Kian only spoke when he was counting the reps for the exercise. He knew this was tough for her today, and yet, he would wait until she was ready to talk about it.

"You think I can't do it, right?" Adalyn asked him after the second set.

Looking up at Adalyn, his eyes very serious, and responded with, "I've always thought ya could do whatever ya wanted."

She sat there, on the floor of the porch, and stared into Kian's eyes. There was nothing in them to indicate that he was patronizing her, or didn't mean exactly what he said. After about a minute, Addy nodded, and started with the next set.

After their session was over, Adalyn sighed with relief. She stayed sitting down, as Kian started to pack up his stuff. His silence made her feel foolish, like she was acting like a child. "Do you think I'm being a jerk?" She asked him, before he left.

Stopping in his tracks, Kian turned around, set his bag back down, then crouched down on the floor so they were face to face. "Ya," He said, and wanted to laugh at the look of shock on her face. "But, I can see what yer trying to accomplish here."

Her feathers sufficiently ruffled, Addy asked, "And what is that?"

Kian cupped her chin, so he knew she would look at him as he spoke. "Yer trying to prove to yourself, and subsequently, everyone else that you will make a full recovery." He smiled, "But yer scared, as ya have every right to be."

"What if I don't want to be scared?" Adalyn asked him, a tear sliding down her cheek.

His heart swelled at the sight of her tears. He wanted so badly to whisk her away and make her feel safe. But, there was no "safe" in this life. He'd learned that lesson two years earlier. Remembering his parents, Kian emotionally stepped back from her. He released her chin, and stood back up. "I'll see ya day after tomorrow."

Adalyn watched him leave and wondered about what secrets Kian Fitzpatrick held back from her. Something made him pull away, but she didn't know what it was.

A few minutes after Kian left, Evelyn came out onto the porch to check on her daughter. Addy was still sitting on the yoga mat, and studying her hands in her lap. "Are you okay?" She asked her daughter, and sat down in a padded wicker chair near the window.

Addy took a minute or two, then looked up at her mom, and smiled, before answering, "I think so."

"Not that I want to add to all the drama we've had piled on us for today," Evelyn started, "but I think I need you to explain why you were messaging Kian on Facebook the other day, pretending to be me."

Addy felt like when she was ten years old, and got caught doing something she wasn't supposed to. "Uh, I don't know," And realized she'd given her mother the same answer when she was ten years old.

Giving her daughter a smirk, Evelyn countered, "Oh, I think you do know why," she set down her cup of tea and leaned forward, "I'm here for you, I support you, Dad supports you, but," she sighed, "I don't want you to start off any relationship under false pretenses."

Her mother had a point, Addy knew it. She nodded in response, and said, "I just wanted to know if he was feeling what I was feeling."

"And what if I said that he was?" Evelyn asked her daughter.

Turning the thought over in her mind, Adalyn smiled, "I'd probably be pretty excited."

Evelyn leaned back in her chair, and asked her daughter, "Do you remember asking me about how Dad made me feel before we got married?"

Thinking hard, Addy actually couldn't remember asking her mother that, and shook her head no.

Sighing, Evelyn said, "I'm not surprised, it was about a week before the accident happened." She smiled, "I think you maybe had an inkling that Tommy wasn't the one for you, but you hadn't admitted it to yourself yet."

Addy nodded, understanding now, that Tommy was most definitely not the right guy for her. It was difficult for her to remember what she found appealing about him in the first place.

"Anyway," Evelyn said, interrupting her daughter's silence, "I told you that every time Dad walked into a room, there were these invisible sparks that flew between us."

Her mother made it sound so beautiful, Adalyn smiled and nodded for her to continue.

Evelyn wanted her daughter to be happy, and told her daughter, "I can feel those same sparks fly between you and Kian every time you're together." Sighing, Evelyn added, "And I can tell you," she pointed to her daughter, "that not everyone gets to have that."

Adalyn sat there and watched her mother get up to leave the room. She had a lot to think about.

Chapter 15

The next day, Adalyn went out with her mom to do some shopping. It was her first real excursion out, and she was a little nervous. Between the rehab center, and her parents' home, she'd been pretty sheltered. Now she had to go out in public, and deal with other people. It was hard to remember that she used to be a model and was on the cover of magazines and had people fussed over her.

They drove up to Pearland, to a strip mall down the main street. It had a great selection of stores, her mother told her.

When Evelyn parked the car, she turned and asked Adalyn, "Are you okay?"

Mustering up her courage, Addy answered, "Yep, let's go."

Hours later, and two trips back to the car to drop off bags, the two of them were sitting in a restaurant and laughing. In the three years that Addy had been asleep, a lot had changed. Fashions were different, people were different, and things were even more hurried.

It was hard for Addy to tell if it was society that changed or just her perception of it. Either way, it was exhilarating and frightening at the same time.

Her mother called her dad while they waited for their food, "She's fine," Evelyn answered him, and smiled at Addy. "We used your credit card," She said, making a face to Addy to show she was teasing Doug. "We'll be home soon, I love you," She added, then ended the call.

Addy laughed, and said, "You shouldn't tease him like that.

Brushing it off, Evelyn chuckled, "It's good for him."

They laughed and talked about clothes for a few more minutes before their food was served. It was hamburgers and milkshakes, and it was heavenly.

"Yum," Addy purred as she tasted her milkshake.

Evelyn laughed, "I don't think I've seen you drink a milkshake since you were fourteen or so."

Trying to remember, Addy nodded, and answered, "I think you're right."

Sitting back, Addy had an epiphany of sorts, "Why did I think that I had to be so skinny and have those pictures?"

Grinning, Evelyn replied, "Because that's what you set your mind on when you were fourteen, and that's what you did."

Adalyn always thought she'd inherited her single-minded determination from her parents. "Your fault," She said to her mother, and stuck her tongue out for good measure.

Laughing, Evelyn almost choked on a French fry. "Lord, I've missed you," She said to her daughter, growing serious for a moment, "Our prayers truly have been answered."

"But not Michelle's," Addy replied, without thinking. When she saw the pain her words caused her mother, Adalyn felt awful, and said, "I'm so sorry, Mom."

Evelyn had to admire that Addy could say what she thought without the burden of uncertainty of how her words would sound. "It's fine, sweetie," She reassured her daughter. "I was just thinking that such a wonderful person shouldn't have been taken so soon."

Trying to be gentle with her words, Addy hesitated. "Maybe it's like Dad said, she did everything she was supposed to do, and helped all the kids she was supposed to help." She reached across the table to hold her mom's hand, and added, "She was just much more efficient about her journey, so it was her time to go."

Tipping her head, Evelyn contemplated the words her daughter chose. "You know," She said to Addy, "you just may be right."

The next day, Adalyn awoke with a new sense of purpose. She'd had a great time with her mother yesterday. No seizures, no stress, just fun, and it made her realize that there was still life to be lived. She wasn't just going to hide from everything that could be difficult or hurt.

Her parents were sitting out in the breakfast nook when she came into the room. The kitchen smelled wonderful, and

Addy smiled as she walked in to see a plate full of freshly baked blueberry muffins. Grabbing one, she walked into the nook, sat down, and started eating the, still warm, muffin.

For the second time in a week, Doug and Evelyn found themselves just sitting there, and staring at their daughter. And, for the second time, Addy asked them, "What?"

Evelyn shook her head, and smiled, saying, "Nothing, you just never used to like blueberries and would never go near muffins because of the carb count."

Sitting back, a grin on her face, Addy replied, "Well, I don't care about the carb count and these blueberries are damn good."

The three of them sat there laughing.

When Kian showed up for Addy's physical therapy session, she was sitting at the table, writing down a list of things she wanted to do.

Kian still wondered what he would be walking into today, with Adalyn, when he arrived at the Phillips' house. Although they hadn't been arguing when he left, he still felt like there was some unresolved issues there. Certainly, he was torn between wanting to hold her and spank her half the time. He could understand her conflicting feelings, for she deserved them. Even knowing what he knew, and having a good feel for what she was going through, he still worried.

Knocking, he pasted on his professional smile. As soon as Adalyn opened the door, his pasted on smile transformed into a genuine one. She looked like a young girl, her hair pulled back into a pony tail, she dressed in a t-shirt, and jean shorts. Her skin, although pale from being in the hospital so long, looked like a piece of sculpture, smooth and long.

"Kian," Addy said with a smile, "Come in." She stepped back and let him inside.

Still smiling, Kian commented, "Well, this is a fine change from the puss ya wore just the other day."

Adalyn giggled at the words, "Yes, and I owe you an apology for the way I acted."

They were next to the dining table, so Kian put down his bag and sat where she motioned, with her sitting down, and facing him.

"I was scared, and just didn't want to admit that there might be something wrong with me." Adalyn explained. "I never should have taken it out on you." Blushing, she added, "And I have to be honest with you, I was the one on my mom's Facebook page the other day, messaging you."

Now it was Kian's turn to blush. "Oh," He answered, not sure what else to say.

Placing her hand over his, that was resting on the table, Adalyn cleared her throat, then said, "I do think that there is something here, between us."

Her words, floored Kian. Here he was, just showin up for an appointment, and now he felt his heart just leap right out of his chest, and flutter through the air like a butterfly. "Do yer parents know?" He asked her, his voice hoarse with nerves and emotion.

Adalyn nodded, "Yes, my mother read the conversation because I'd closed out of Facebook before you answered my last question, and she saw it." She squeezed his hand, "She said that you and I have the same spark between us that she and my dad have."

Kian was touched by Evelyn Phillips' understanding of how things were. It wasn't every parent who would think that way. Lord knew, he was still questioning whether having these feelings for Adalyn was a conflict of interest for him. But, she was willing to be honest for him, so he should do the same. "I used to talk to ya, when ya were sleepin." He smiled softly, "I would tell ya about my day, my problems, my life, as we did yer exercises."

Leaning back, Adalyn let the information sink in. Perhaps it explained why she was so at ease with Kian, she knew everything about him really, even if she couldn't remember it. "Did I ever respond?"

Kian shook his head no, and answered, "Not until ya started wakin up and the nurses were there." He squeezed her hand gently now, "Oh, it was such a lift to my heart to see ya open yer eyes."

The way he spoke, made Addy feel as if she were in some poem. It was beautiful and sincere. "I'm glad."

Neither of them knew what to say then, so they sat there, the atmosphere ripe with tension.

Adalyn was the first to break the silence, saying, "So, I'm hoping that you'll do two things for me."

Something in the way she was looking, mischievous, like a she-devil herself, had Kian on edge, and asking, "Now, what would those be?"

"First," Adalyn began, "I'd like you to help me get up those stairs," she pointed behind her to the stairs.

Kian didn't know where the stairs led, but he was intrigued, and answered, "Of course."

They both stood up, and Kian stepped to her side, to support her weight as they made it up the split level staircase.

Stairs, for some reason, were still a challenge for Addy. She'd never even attempted these since they were a full flight.

As they reached the top of the stairs, both Kian and Adalyn sighed. It was a huge loft area, with pitched ceiling areas, but lit up by two huge sets of windows; one on the front of the house, and the other on the side.

"Wow," Adalyn said, "this is so cool!"

Kian looked at her, and asked, "Ya didn't know what was up here then?"

Addy shook her head, "Mom just said they used it for storage."

Sure enough, there were piles of boxes here and there. Some were marked with holiday titles, denoting that they were most likely decorations. Some just said miscellaneous.

Standing up, and slowly turning around, Addy thought it was just perfect. She turned to Kian and said, "I think we should paint it."

Okay, as if the day's conversations weren't strange enough, now Adalyn wanted him to help her paint a room that her parents didn't even use. "Why?" He asked her.

Smiling slyly, as she looked over at Kian, Adalyn answered, "Isn't it darling?" She stepped in front of him, and pointed at the space in front of the windows, "Wouldn't that be a perfect sitting area to read in, or just chat?" She asked him.

Nodding, Kian answered, "I guess."

"Oh, Men!" Adalyn said in exasperation. "No sense of adventure."

"Excuse me!" Kian responded, appalled at her choice of words, "I'm an Irishman, we are the epitome of adventure! We invented Leprechauns, and tell the best stories ever!"

Trying to bite back laughter, Adalyn tried to soothe his bruised ego with, "I'm sorry, I didn't mean to insult you."

Kian was standing there, deciding whether or not to forgive her, when Mr. and Mrs. Phillips came upstairs.

Evelyn said, "I thought I heard voices up here, I thought you two were supposed to be doing physical therapy?" She asked her daughter, the motherly gleam in her eyes.

"We did," Addy rushed out, "Kian and I came up the whole flight of stairs."

Doug shook his head, and commented, "I don't think that counts."

Waving her hand, Evelyn piped up with, "It does count, a little."

Knowing that his wife ran the show, Doug smiled, then asked, "Uh, is there a reason we're all standing up in a mostly semi-empty room that nobody is using?"

That was an easy one, as far as Adalyn was concerned. She smiled sweetly at her dad, answering, "I'm going to try and make it into my own space, if that's okay with you and Mom?"

At first, Evelyn was going to say no. There was no railing, and her motherly instinct was to protect her daughter. But then, she saw how hopeful Addy looked. As if her daughter could already envision the space. It was a goal, and Addy certainly needed a few of those right now. "I don't see why not, do you Doug?" She asked her husband.

Looking from his wife, to his daughter, and then to Kian, who frankly, looked as confused as he himself was, Doug just shrugged, and answered, "Whatever you want."

Adalyn stepped forward, and hugged her dad tightly. "Oh thank you," She said, and smiled brightly at her mom. "And Kian said he'd help me."

All three sets of eyes turned to Kian, who smiled blankly. He didn't technically agree to this, but if it meant time spent with Adalyn, he'd do it. "I'd have ta do it after my appointments, and on the weekends." He said, trying to sound as though he was calling the shots, which he knew he was most definitely not doing.

Addy smiled, "That's fine, I'll work on my other things during the day, and we can work on this a few nights a week, and I'll make sure that I get in my physical therapy too, and get stronger, so you won't feel like you're doing all the work."

Her attitude, and tone, were contagious. There was no way Kian could resist it when she smiled like that. And, if he thought he was in trouble before, he knew it with certainty now. The woman had him wrapped around her finger like a piece of yarn, he was sure of it.

The four of them went downstairs, with Kian and Adalyn turning to go out onto the porch to do some physical therapy in the time Kian had left before his next appointment, and Doug and Evelyn went into the kitchen.

Doug sat at the bar as his wife put on the teakettle. He asked her, "You know that we weren't planning on using that space, and it may turn out that Addy can't really use it either?"

Leaning on the counter, in front of her husband, "Yes, but I saw how happy she was to have a goal, and how happy she was to have Kian be a part of it."

Not too fond of possibly losing his little girl to another man, so soon after she woke up, Doug had his reservations. But, looking at his happy wife, he knew that he'd give them all whatever they needed. "I love you," He told Evelyn.

"Oh, Doug," She said, and walked over to stand in front of him, "I love you too."

Chapter 16

So, for the next week, Adalyn did whatever was required of her. She wanted to show everyone that she was willing to be a "good girl" if it meant getting to do what she wanted.

The day after Kian's visit, she sat down with her parents and talked to them about the list she'd compiled. It was of things she wanted to do, some of them were fanciful, like ice skating, or visiting Rome, and some were realistic, like continuing her education, and getting her driver's license.

They talked for a long time, prioritizing what she should be working towards, what they needed to discuss with her doctors, and what she could do in the meantime.

She received a letter in the mail, from her bank in Dallas, and was astonished to find that there was still money in an account she'd completely forgotten about. And, as it turned out, an account that she hadn't put Tommy on.

Showing her parents the letter, she was a little confused. "How did they know to send this to me?" She asked them.

Evelyn sighed, "Well, I think I told you about the legal battle we had with Tommy, when you'd first had the accident."

"Yes," Addy answered, and sat down at the breakfast bar.

Seeing her husband nod, in support, Evelyn explained, "Well, we sort of got a lawyer, when all of that stuff with the accounts was going on."

Addy nodded, and said, "Okay."

"Well," Evelyn blushed, "we sort of instructed the lawyer to make sure that some of your assets were hidden from him."

Her eyebrows raised, Addy started to smile slowly. The situation was becoming clearer, and she blew her mom a kiss, saying, "Oh, you are a sly one, and I really appreciate it."

There was a good feeling knowing that you were getting over on someone. Normally, Addy wouldn't be vindictive, but in this case, she would make the exception. "Well," She said to her parents, "Since I still have some wealth, I insist on taking on the renovating costs myself and paying for any of my education costs, as soon as the doctors say I'm fit to go back to school."

Doug smiled, and asked Adalyn, "Have you decided what you want to go back for?"

Adalyn nodded, "Yep, I'm going to be a teacher."

Her parents didn't seem as surprised as she assumed they'd be. Of course, Michelle had something to do with her decision. Her cousin never wasted any time living, and her example taught Adalyn to do the same.

"Teaching?" Doug asked, and nodded. "What subject were you thinking of?"

Adalyn shrugged, and answered, "I'm not exactly sure." She looked at her mother, and smiled. "I've checked into some colleges and a lot of my credits will transfer, when you do your student teaching, they can put you with different age groups so I'll be able to find what works for me."

Evelyn said, "It seems like you've worked a lot of this out."

"I have," Adalyn responded, "and I'm sure this is the way I want to go."

Evelyn's phone rang then, and she answered it, "Hello."

Addy watched her mother's face turn from one of happiness into one of repulsion. She started to worry when her mother's eyes darted over to her father.

Reaching out, the phone still in her hand, Evelyn said, "It's for you......it's Tommy."

Surprised that Tommy would be calling for her, Adalyn took the phone from her mother, and said, "Hello."

"I'd like for us to meet," Tommy said, not wasting any time.

Adalyn felt irritated that he thought he could just order her around. "I'm fairly sure we don't have anything to discuss unless you're willing to give back MY money to me."

Evelyn covered her mouth with her hand, to hide her laughter, and Doug's eyebrows just rose in surprise.

Tommy, not used to having people stand up to his bullying tactics, let his voice raise, "I would like to see you."

Smiling benignly at her parents, to hide her growing anger, she said, in an overly calm voice, "Tom," she knew he hated being called that, "I think if you really wanted to see me, you would've done so while I was lying in a hospital bed for three years." After that, she simply hit disconnect, and handed the phone back to her mother.

Evelyn did allow herself to laugh once Adalyn was off the phone. "Oh, my Lord, did he get mad?" She asked.

"You know Tommy, he just pitches a fit until he gets what he wants, and he's not about to get what he wants, if it has anything to do with me." She sat back and folded her arms, to emphasize her point.

Doug grimaced, and asked, "What the hell did you see in him and what the hell does Jeni see in him?"

Looking over at her father, her face serious, Addy answered with, "You know, I'm not sure I want to tell my father, but let's just say, I'm over it now."

Again, Evelyn started to laugh. Their daughter was growing stronger in ways that none of them could have imagined.

They sat at the table, forgetting about Tommy and started discussing what kinds of things Adalyn wanted to do.

The next day, Adalyn had an appointment with Dr. Cooper, and she asked her mom if her dad could take her. Evelyn said, "Of course," but did look a little surprised.

"So," Doug asked as they buckled up their seat belts, "Why are we ditching your mother?"

Smiling brightly, Addy answered, "We're not ditching her; we're just spending some father-daughter time together."

Pulling out of the driveway, Doug smiled, and responded, "It didn't work when you were fifteen, and it won't work now."

His insight made Adalyn laugh. "Dad, you know me too well."

Doug laughed as they made their way down the road, "I do, even after all that's happened."

His words were met with a pregnant silence.

"I'm sorry, sweetie," Doug said quickly, trying to smooth over the awkward moment.

Addy sighed, "Dad, don't be sorry." She looked over and smiled, "We can't pretend the accident and coma didn't happen."

Nodding, Doug agreed. "I know," He told her, "but I'm not sure what to say sometimes."

"Dad," Adalyn replied, "I'm not sure what to say sometimes, and I was the one who went through it."

Her openness made Doug respect her even more. "Let's make a pact that we'll just treat it like any other thing."

That made sense to Addy, "That's cool," she answered, and then asked, "And would you mind taking me driving soon so I can get my license reinstated."

Shaking his head, Doug answered, "I knew it!" But nodded anyway, and said, "Of course."

By the time they reached the rehabilitation center, Adalyn was smiling widely.

Dr. Cooper came into the exam room, and noticed a change in Adalyn from just the other day. This was a new woman, mentally speaking. "Well," He looked at her chart, "How are we doing?"

"Great!" Adalyn replied.

He smiled at her, and asked, "So, what's new?"

Tilting her head, Adalyn pretended to look like she was thinking, then answered, "Well, I've made a list of things I need or want to do, I got to tell off my ex-fiancé, my parents are awesome, supportive people, and......oh by the way, I think I might be falling in love with Kian."

Her last words had Dr. Cooper stopping his forward progress, and smile. "Well, that's interesting news," He said.

Smiling smugly, Addy just crossed her arms across her chest, and remained silent.

Dr. Cooper proceeded with his exam, checking her breathing, using a light to check her eyes, and asking a few other questions. There didn't seem to be any evidence of further seizures, and they were both relieved to hear it.

"Now, when do I get to start driving?" Addy asked him as she waited for him to input the information into his computer.

Looking over his shoulder, Dr. Cooper sighed, "I will give you the all clear after I see you in a month, if you've had no seizures or any other complications, you'll be good to go."

Adalyn sighed in disappointment. She'd hoped her plans would proceed on a faster track, but she had to remember, she'd just "woken up" only weeks earlier.

Spinning his chair around, so he was now facing Adalyn, Dr. Cooper explained. "Your reflexes and strength aren't back yet. I don't want to upset you or tear down your excitement, I just know that we can't be too hasty when it comes to this."

Nodding, she said, "I know."

Dr. Cooper patted her hand, "We'll get you up and running soon enough, I think for now, maybe you should just enjoy the fact that you don't have to work and drive around," he winked playfully, "People are really nuts on the road."

His comment had Adalyn laughing.

"Out!" He commanded, with no real bite to his tone. "I'll see you in a month."

Giving him a salute, Addy hopped off the table and headed out. She smiled at her dad when she came out, saying, "Looks good so far."

They left the center to go home, and about ten minutes in, Adalyn noticed her father was taking a different route home than the one they took to get there. "Are we stopping off?" She asked him.

Smiling at his daughter, Doug said, "Yes," but was quiet after that.

Twenty minutes later, Adalyn was laughing again. "Really?" She asked her father. They pulled up into the local ice cream place.

Addy was practically dancing her way inside, and was all smiles as they placed their orders.

"I can't believe you thought of this," She said to her dad, as they sat down to wait for their orders to be delivered.

Doug smiled at his daughter, he loved her exuberance. "I can," He replied in a droll tone, "Your mother never lets me come here, she says it's not good for me."

Nodding, Adalyn countered with, "So now I'm in coercion with you about hiding your secret ice cream obsession from Mom?"

Looking around, as if they were spies on a covert mission, Doug replied, "If you want me to take you driving......."

They chatted and laughed while they ate their ice cream. Both of them used the bathrooms to make sure there was no evidence of their food indiscretion, then went home.

Evelyn came out onto the porch as they pulled into the garage. She waved to them as they started up to the door, and asked, "How did it go?"

Addy shot a look to her father and winked, before turning back to her mother, and answering, "Good, but I have to wait a month before Dr. Cooper will give me the all clear to get my license back."

Nodding, Evelyn hugged her daughter quickly, then turned to kiss her husband. She stepped back to go into the house, and commented, "Next time, you might want to do a better job of getting the mint and chocolate taste gone before you come home from eating ice cream."

Stopping mid-stride, Addy turned around, saw her mother's knowing look, her father blushing in shame, and broke out into laughter. "Oh, she's good," She said as she turned to continue into the kitchen.

Doug replied, "You have no idea," and winked at his wife before following her.

They sat down at the breakfast table, and discussed Addy's appointment, what she thought her next move would be, and her plans for the upstairs loft.

Doug groaned. "I feel a sore back coming on," He said playfully, and got up to pour himself a cup of iced tea.

"Oh, don't be so dramatic," Evelyn said to him. "It will be fun for Addy, and give her a project."

Nodding, Adalyn injected, "Well, don't forget Kian, he'll be helping me the most, Dad, you won't end up with a sore back."

Looking at his daughter, Doug answered dryly, "Yes, but he will."

Chapter 17

Kian arrived for their session the next day, and felt very light-hearted. He'd been thinking about Adalyn non-stop since he left her a few days before, and now he felt like they had turned a corner of sorts, and they might be headed in a good direction.

After knocking, and being greeted by Mr. Phillips, Kian was showed into the kitchen, where both Adalyn and Mrs. Phillips were.

"Good morning, Kian," Evelyn said in a bright tone.

Smiling, Kian answered, "And to ya' as well, Mrs. Phillips."

Adalyn stood up and asked him, "Would it be okay if we took a walk as part of our therapy session?"

He couldn't find any good reason that they shouldn't walk, so he answered, "Sure, lead the way," and gestured for her to precede him. He gave a quick wave to Mr. and Mrs. Phillips, out of respect, and then followed Adalyn to the back door.

They left the house, with Adalyn only needing minimal help to navigate the stairs on the porch, and started walking toward the back yard.

"My parents bought this lot because it was very deep." She started to explain as they walked, "I've been meaning to explore it, but haven't had the energy until now."

Kian nodded, but didn't say anything. He didn't feel as though he had to, really.

Adalyn found herself being very nervous. She and Kian had all but said the words that they felt something for one another. But, she found that now, the words were harder than she imagined them to be. "So, I saw Dr. Cooper yesterday," She blurted out, to break the ice.

"Aye," Kian answered, "I heard all about it from Mrs. Wilkins, how ya just look fabulous!"

His impersonation of Mrs. Wilkins made her laugh. "Yes," She started, "I said something to him yesterday, and he didn't seem very surprised by it."

Kian was looking ahead, out of habit, for any obstacles that might impede her progression, so he wasn't facing her, and only responded with, "And what would that be that yer tellin Dr. Cooper?"

Adalyn stopped, and waited for Kian to look at her, "I told him that I think I'm falling in love with you."

A whisper of wind could have blown Kian over; he was so surprised by her words. It wasn't as if he didn't know she felt something for him, it was just the confident way in which she used those words when speaking to him that blew him away. "So ya think so, hey?" He asked her, trying to buy time to get his brain to start functioning again.

"Yes," She answered him.

Stepping forward, so he was only inches from her, Kian framed her face with his palms, and said, "Well, tis a good thing then because I'm feelin like I'm about to burst, my heart is so full when I'm around ya."

He couldn't have put it any better, as far as Adalyn was concerned. "Well, then," She said, and left the words hanging.

"Well, then," He mimicked her, and leaned in for a kiss.

As their lips met, a tremble worked its way through Adalyn's body. It wasn't because she was cold, it was the settling inside of her, the feeling of being exactly in the right place, just then.

Kian kept the kiss light. He didn't want to overwhelm Adalyn with his wanton need, and there was plenty of that building up inside of him. There was also a need for him to tread lightly in this, the physical aspect of their relationship. But it was difficult because, even as he thought it, the feeling of her lips joined with his was taking him to heights that would make any man feel dizzy.

Even though Kian pulled back first, much to Adalyn's disappointment, she was smiling.

When Kian opened his eyes, to a smiling Adalyn, he whispered, "And aren't you a sight beyond all."

Sighing, Addy responded, "You are such a poet."

"Yeah," Kian replied, "I'm Irish."

He seemed to just charm the giggles right out of Addy, and she was grateful for his talent to do so. It was so easy, just to walk and talk with Kian. "I won't pretend that I'm not a little scared, because it's been over three years since I've even kissed a man." She looked up into his eyes, "But that was fantastic!"

Oh, she did wonders for his heart, and the rest of him too, for that matter. Now, if only he could tell her......

Adalyn remembered the phone call from Tommy, and brought it up, "I forgot to tell you, my ex-fiancé called me yesterday."

Those words had Kian's shackles up quickly. "And what did that no good, gom have to say for himself?" He asked her as they started walking again.

Sneaking a peek at Kian, Adalyn commented, "I don't think I want to know what a gom is, but he wanted to see me."

Now Kian stopped, the anger inside of him building. "What fer?"

"He didn't say, and I didn't ask, other than to comment that if he wanted to return the money he stole from me, then that was fine, other than that, I didn't think we had anything to discuss." Addy told him, still feeling good about her new attitude.

Kian nodded, "Good lass," he said, and followed up by asking, "What do ya mean, money he stole?"

Adalyn told him about what her mother relayed to her; about how after the accident, Tommy wanted to take her off of life support, and then how he took her money since she had put him on her bank account. Kian couldn't believe it. How could someone who said he loved her, do that to her? If you loved someone, you owed them respect. Kian realized that he too, owed Adalyn the respect of being honest. "I've got something I want to tell you," He started then stopped when they heard a car screeching to a halt in the driveway.

They'd turned around, to head back to the house, and saw an expensive sedan come roaring into the driveway. Adalyn instinctively, held on to Kian's arm. She was glad she did when she saw Tommy get out of the vehicle.

He slammed the car door, and glared at the house for a minute or so. When he started to round the vehicle, Adalyn yelled out, "What are you doing here?"

Turning, Tommy caught sight of Adalyn, with that Irish idiot who'd thrown him out of her hospital room. "Ahh, still slumming it, I see," His words dripped with sarcasm.

"Ah, still a narcissistic ass, I see," Adalyn said with a smile.

Tommy let the comment go, "I chose to not take no for an answer," was his counter.

Kian was a half-step in front of Adalyn, in case he needed to "help" this gimp if he decided to overstep. He was quiet, preferring to let Adalyn handle him, and doing a splendid job of it, she was.

"What do you want, Tommy?" Adalyn asked as they neared his vehicle.

Tommy tried to smile sweetly, and answered, "I think we have some business to discuss." He was making it clear that he wanted to speak to her alone.

Shaking her head, Adalyn replied, "We have no business to discuss unless, as I told you yesterday, it's to get the money you took from me."

He smiled, and said, "That was a joint account."

Getting fed up with his little tantrums, Adalyn decided to take a jab or two herself. "There was almost half a million in that account, from my modeling jobs, and there is nothing that proves you contributed anything to that account."

Shocked, by the amount of money Adalyn had, Kian just stood there. To his way of thinking, the gob needed to return the money, and leave Adalyn be. Of course, men like Tommy didn't do the right thing.

"It was a joint account," He responded, in a dry tone.

Adalyn could see her parents standing on the porch, and put her hand up to let them know it was okay. "What "business" did you want to discuss?"

Tommy was reluctant at first, then decided to just spit it out. "A couple of television shows and magazines have contacted me and offered a good amount of money for our story."

Completely flabbergasted at his lack of anything resembling a reasonable human being, she yelled, "Our story? There is no our story, there is you, taking my money and trying to shut off the machines that were keeping me alive." She poked at his chest, "Is that the story you want me to tell?" Pushing forward, and smiling on the inside that he was actually stepping back, she went on, "How about I tell them how I caught you in bed with my best friend, Jeni, and, in my emotional state, lost control of my car?"

Kian watched as the man turned three different shades of red. "I was just thinking that we could make some money. Clearly you're not working right now, I'm sure your parents could use some extra cash….."

Adalyn didn't even let him finish, "You son-of-a-bitch!" She stepped forward, and slapped him in the face. "How dare you!" She railed at him, "How dare you come here, to my family's home, and insult us this way!" Giving him a final push, she said, "If you aren't in that car, which by the way, I'm sure I bought, and out of the driveway in one minute, I'm sure my dad won't mind calling the police."

His mouth clenched in anger, Tommy retorted, "You wouldn't dare."

"Maybe she wouldn't, but I would," Doug Phillips yelled, "Now get the hell off of my property!"

The three of them turned to see Adalyn's parents had come out onto the back porch.

Without another word, Tommy stomped over to the car door, opened it, and tore out of the driveway.

As the car sped off down the road, Adalyn tried to get her temper under control. She was grateful that Kian had remained silent through the whole episode, but now she was embarrassed. She turned to him, tears flooding her eyes, and whispered, "I'm sorry you had to see that."

Taking her into his arms, "Oh, don't ya worry now, but I'll tell ya, I don't really plan on makin ya mad any time soon."

His light tone made her laugh in spite of her racing heart. "See, you better not mess with the bull, or you'll get the horns."

Kian rubbed her back, trying to soothe. "Let's go inside and have us a nice shot of whiskey," He said, and turned to lead her inside the house.

Evelyn came down the steps of the porch to meet them. She gave Adalyn a tight hug, and asked her, "Are you okay?"

Nodding, Addy replied, "Yes," and tried to calm herself, "But if he comes back here, he won't be."

Her comment made the other three chuckle. They knew she meant it.

Doug clapped Kian on the back as they went inside. "Interesting day," He commented.

Kian wasn't sure if Mr. Phillips meant their kiss, the run-in with Adalyn's ex, or both. He nodded, and replied, "Yes, sir."

The four of them sat down in the breakfast nook, with Addy sitting closest to the windows. She didn't participate in the others' conversation about Tommy and his gall, instead, she looked outside, hoping that the serenity of the landscape would help her relax.

"Are ya really okay?" Kian leaned over, and asked Adalyn softly.

Looking at him, a smile forming, Adalyn responded, "I am, really," she winked at him. "Thank you," She said.

Evelyn sat down, after placing four shot glasses down, and a bottle of the whiskey Kian mentioned earlier. "What?" She asked her husband, when she saw the surprised look on his face. "We deserve this."

Kian nodded, "Yeah, we do."

Doug poured, and they all lifted their glasses, "To starting over," Adalyn spoke.

The whiskey was warm as it worked its way down her throat. She was honestly surprised that her parents kept much alcohol in the house, as they'd never been big drinkers. She asked, "Did you start drinking after my accident?" And watched three sets of eyes on her.

"Uh, no," Doug answered, and smiled, "It's not all about you." And they all laughed, as he poured another round.

After the second shot, Doug answered, "Actually, Kian gave me this bottle last Christmas."

Nodding, Kian confirmed, "Ah, I remember that alright. There is nothin so comfortin as a good woman, and a good whiskey," He said, repeating one of his father's sayings.

Evelyn piped in with, "I'll drink to that."

Adalyn looked around the table, and realized that the three most important people in the world, to her, were right here. She felt humbled, and very lucky, and said a silent prayer in thanks.

That evening, after his other appointments, Kian came back to the Phillips' house. This was the day he and Adalyn were supposed to start on the upstairs loft project. He'd received a fair amount of teasing from Adalyn's father regarding a sore back, but he was willing to do whatever it took to make Adalyn happy.

Adalyn was sitting out on the porch as he pulled in. She stood when he parked, and got out of his car. "Is there somethin wrong?" He asked her.

Shaking her head no, Adalyn came down the steps and met him on the sidewalk that led from the driveway to the house. "I was hoping for another kiss," She said, smiling shyly at him.

"Now that's a request I'll be happy man to fulfill," Kian replied, and took her into his arms.

This kiss was a little more……..everything. Longer, for sure, but there was more of a connection between them. Addy felt it, all the way down to her toes; that beating pulse of need. When the kiss ended, she sighed. "Now that was worth waiting for," She said before leading the way into the house.

Chapter 18

As summer dug its heels into South Texas, so started Adalyn's fall into love. It was amazing, to feel so elated when you knew you were going to see someone, and that they were so excited to see you too.

It had been weeks since Kian kissed her during their walk, and it made Adalyn wonder if she was lacking in some area. Mostly, she suspected it was because they were never alone. Her parents were in the house and she wanted to believe that Kian was just being respectful.

Today, they were discussing paint schemes. There were now half walls built up around the stair case, all of the miscellaneous stuff in the boxes were organized, and tucked into the adjoining attic space, and the floors were refinished and shone in the bright afternoon light.

Kian was standing near the set of windows, at the front of the room, and Adalyn blurted out, "Why haven't you kissed me since we took that walk?"

Slowly turning around, Kian was surprised that it took her this long to ask. As they were getting to know one another, Kian was quickly learning that Adalyn didn't waste time on certain things. He smiled at her, and answered, "I've been waitin."

"For what?" Adalyn asked him, setting down the paint samples.

Kian walked over to where she stood, looking into her beautiful eyes, so full of questions. "For us to be alone, and to know that ya were sure," He said.

"I'm sure," Addy whispered, "that I want you to kiss me again."

He leaned down, to fulfill the request, and then they heard Evelyn and Doug coming up the stairs. Kian stepped back quickly, a smile in his eyes.

As Evelyn stepped up into the loft, she got a look at her daughter, and Kian, and stopped. "Uh, Doug," She said, "I think we need to go to the store."

Doug almost ran into his wife's back, "What?" He asked, "I thought you wanted to look at color samples?"

Turning around, giving her husband the look that said, 'Do what I say!' she went back downstairs, practically dragging Doug with her. "We'll be back soon," She yelled up the stairs, and was still nodding at her grumbling husband as she grabbed her purse and led him outside to the car.

Both Kian and Adalyn waited to hear the front door close, then started laughing.

"Your ma, she's a sly one," Kian spoke first.

Stepping back toward him, Adalyn nodded. "She always told me that when I found the person I wanted to be with most, I would know it."

Curious, Kian asked, "Did ya know it when you met that Tommy fella?"

Shaking her head no, Adalyn answered, "I can't begin to tell you how much time I've spent wondering what I ever saw in him."

"And now?" Kian asked her, taking a step toward her.

Only a few inches from him, Adalyn said, "I think I was desperate to feel a part of something."

Kian nodded. "Ya never talk of that modeling stuff ya did."

Her mind scattered, Adalyn feeling uneasy. "Why would I want to?" She asked him.

The moment of awareness was gone, Kian felt it. She was defensive now, but he didn't personally feel like they could move forward until the past was settled. Some of that kept him from getting closer to her, he knew it. "Because, it's part of who ya were." He returned, and led her over to a bench to sit down.

Adalyn followed his lead, the logical part of her mind knew he was right. She sat down, and turned to face him. "Okay, when I was about sixteen, my mom and I went to a luncheon for a local church in Houston." She started, "The organizers asked me to model some clothes, since a clothing company was one of the sponsors."

"Was it fun?" He asked her.

Addy was surprised by the question, and thought back to that time. "Yes, it really was." She smiled, "Anyway, so one of the reps from the clothing company liked me I guess, and they called my parents the next week, asking if they could sign me to a contract."

Kian nodded. "So that was the beginnin?" He asked.

"Yes," Adalyn answered. "And it was a whole lot of fun then, traipsing around the state, doing shows, doing the photo sessions, and making friends."

He looked into her eyes, "And then?"

Sighing, Adalyn continued, "And then some big names got a look at me, and everything changed." She looked down at her hands, "Instead of staying in Texas, I was seventeen and flying around the world."

"I saw ya on the cover of a more than a few magazines," Kian told her.

It was hard not to blush, thinking about some of those covers. She looked twice her age and exuded sex. "I didn't really care for them, but they made me a lot of money."

The sadness in her voice made Kian think she felt stuck in that life. "And then that goff, Tommy? Where did he come in?"

Adalyn shook her head, "He was a rep for a company that I was doing a modeling shoot for." She looked out the window for a minute, before going on, "He was sophisticated, and he made me feel protected," she looked up at Kian, and said, "And now, I realize he pegged me as someone he could control."

Kian was amazed that she could analyze the relationship so well. "And you found him and Jeni?"

Shaking her head, Adalyn answered, "I don't remember anything from the day of the accident. That's what my parents told me." She smiled, "But I'll be thankful for that day because, although it hurt the people who love me, it let me escape the unhappiness of what my life would've been with him."

"Do ya believe that?" Kian asked her.

She'd done hours of thinking, analyzing, talking to Christie, her therapist, and talking to her parents, and she was now sure that Tommy was most definitely not the right man for her. Nodding at Kian, she said, "Oh yes."

His mind a little more at ease, Kian felt better. He certainly didn't want to rush her into anything, especially after seeing that arse of a Tommy do his number on her. "I'd like to kiss ya," He said, feeling that jittery feeling in his belly.

Giving Kian a look of frustration, "Now, you want to kiss me?" She asked sarcastically. "Well, maybe I'll make YOU wait now."

He knew she was kidding him, but it was cute. "Oh, so now yer gonna make me wait?" He asked jokingly.

"Well, actually," Adalyn said, embarrassed, "I'm worried that my mouth is dry and I really don't want to kiss you if I have bad breath."

Her candor made him smile. He stood up, dug out some gum out of his pants pocket, handed her a piece, and popped one into his own mouth. "Now," He exaggerated his chewing, "ya've got no excuses."

Smiling, and chewing her gum, Adalyn retorted, "I can't kiss you now, I'm chewing gum," She made a little bubble with her tongue, and popped it to emphasize her point.

Reaching down, Kian scooped her up into his arms, "Oh, yer the devil, woman, keeping me waitin now, as you are."

Giggling, Addy winked at him. "I'll tell you what," she smirked, "I'll kiss you, if you help me pick out a color to paint these plain, white walls.

Kian plopped down on the bench, beside her, and grabbed up the paint sample papers off the floor. "Fine," He said, pretending to be pouting.

When Addy's parents returned, her mother made a lot of noise, Adalyn sat upstairs, laughing. "Someone would have to be in a coma to not here them," She remarked as her mother slowly came up the stairs.

"Not nice," Kian hissed, then smiled, and said, "Hello, Mrs. Phillips."

"Evelyn, please," She said to Kian. "What did you decide to do, or have you been busy with other things?" She directed the question to Addy.

Smiling up at her mother, Addy said, "Well, I'm twenty-four years old, so I don't think I need the talk, Mom."

Shaking her hand at Addy, she whispered, "If your father saw what I saw, he'd be growling at Kian."

"I would not!" Doug said from behind his wife. Unlike her, he'd been quiet, while coming up the stairs. "It's not like either Kian or Addy have kept their feelings under wraps, Evelyn."

Seeing the look on her mother's face, made Addy laugh again. "No secrets in this house," She announced to Kian, who was also laughing.

Sighing, Evelyn plopped down next to Addy. "Well," She said, "since everyone knows everything, I guess I should tell you that we were at the store, and we saw Jeni's parents."

The statement had Adalyn's head jerking up, a frown on her face, she asked, "Did they say anything?"

Doug leaned against the half wall, and answered, "They said hello. They're down here visiting friends, and they seemed really surprised to see us."

Kian just kept quiet. From what he understood, Jeni and Adalyn were friends since high school. He didn't want to interrupt, or upset Adalyn with any comments he might make.

"That's nice that they talked to you," Adalyn said.

Evelyn looked at her daughter, and asked her, "Are you upset about Jeni being with Tommy?"

It took Adalyn very little time to think about it, she answered, "I actually pity her. He's an ass."

Doug tried to cover his laughter with clearing his throat.

Evelyn smiled at Addy, and gave her a quick hug. "You know, I think I really like the woman you've become. You speak your mind and hold nothing back."

Kian couldn't help it, he asked, "So, Adalyn wasn't always this brazen?"

Now, Doug snorted, "NO," he shrugged at the severe look his wife shot him. "No offense Addy, but you were pretty sheltered, and being around all those models." He looked at Kian, and added, "Very insecure girls."

Adalyn nodded, "Yes, I agree with you, Dad." She said.

It felt odd to Kian, them sitting here, and talking about Adalyn as if she were two different people. But, then again, she really was, in a lot of ways. Maybe people had a kind of "reboot" button, and Adalyn's had been pushed.

"Did you decide on a color?" Evelyn asked, breaking up the momentary silence. She didn't want to think about her little girl's heartbreak.

Switching gears, Adalyn picked up 2 pieces of paper, "We've narrowed it down to these two, help us pick."

Fifteen minutes later, Kian and Doug were on their way to Home Depot to pick up the paint the women decided on.

As he pulled onto the road, Doug said, "I wanted to thank you again, for helping."

"Mr. Phillips, I mean Doug," Kian corrected himself, "I think we both know that what I feel for yer daughter, tis more than either of us thought would be possible."

Smiling at Kian, "No wonder why women fall for your Irish guys, the way you put things, it's like poetry."

Kian chuckled, "I don't think my ma would agree, she always said the Irish men were a bit too flowery with the words."

Doug asked, "Where do your parents live?"

"They're both gone," Kian answered, "two years, it's been now."

His smile fading, Doug offered, "I'm so sorry," to Kian.

Nodding, Kian returned, "Thank you, tis for the better as they were both sufferin'."

Not wanting to pry, but wondering what he meant, Doug asked, "Were they ill?"

"No," Kian answered, "they were both injured in a car accident."

It didn't take Doug very long to correlate a few things in his mind, and he didn't speak for the rest of the drive. Instead, he wondered about this man, and how, even after knowing what he did, how he still managed to see Adalyn in such a special way.

They went into Home Depot, and went to the paint department. Doug ordered 3 gallons of the selected color, and they waited for the salesclerk to mix it up.

Kian felt like something wasn't right, and asked, "Did my tellin you bout my parents upset ya?"

Doug was surprised, and gave a quick, "Oh no, it was just that," he wasn't sure how to word it, "since your parents were in an accident, and so was Addy, I was just surprised that you were so open with her."

Open wasn't a word that Kian would use, but he appreciated Adalyn's father's explanation. "What Adalyn has done, is nothin short of a miracle, prompted by, what I'll be considerin, as her strong spirit, and yer strong love."

"I could be a manly man, and disagree with you, but I don't." He smiled at the clerk as he handed them the cans of paint. "Her accident shook us to the core." He explained, as they walked through the store, toward the checkout. "Evelyn was inconsolable, understandably, and I just wanted her closer."

They found a line, and waited.

Doug continued, "And when that ass wanted to shut off the machines, I really thought Evelyn was going to strangle him." He clenched his jaw at the thought, then went on, "But we were her parents, and her family, and we prayed."

"And tanks be to the good Lord, for ya," Kian offered.

Shaking his head, "No," he said, "Thanks be to the good Lord for Adalyn."

Smiling, Kian replied, "I can't be disagreein with that now."

They moved up, and checked out.

On the way back to the house, they didn't really talk, just enjoyed the silence. Each of them, had a lot to think about.

Chapter 19

A few days later, they were all standing in the loft, admiring all of their hard work. None of them were professional painters, so it took a lot longer than it probably should have, but it was done, and beautiful.

"It looks like sunshine," Addy sighed.

Kian looked at her, "And yet, it dims in comparison to yer sweet smile."

She looked at him, smiling, "I love the way you say things."

Doug chuckled, and asked his wife, "Evelyn, why don't we go downstairs and make some dinner?"

Not needing to be prodded, Evelyn answered, "I think that's a great idea, bye." She looked over at her daughter, and Kian, and they hadn't noticed anything but one another.

Kian knew that her parents left, but he couldn't tear his eyes from her face. It was beautiful, even with the little smudge of paint on her cheek. "I see ya up here," He started, "with children, readin to them."

Adalyn looked around the room, trying to see it how he did. She shrugged, "I've never really thought of that," she said to him.

Stepping forward, Kian placed his hands on her arms, absently rubbing them, and smiled. "Ya know," He said, "we're done paintin……"

"And you think you deserve a kiss now?" She asked, feigning innocence.

Kian nodded, "Yes, sweet lass," he pulled her closer, "kiss my lips and make me happy."

All Adalyn could do was nod, and then she leaned up and brought her lips to his. As their bodies connected, physically, she shifted emotionally. It was if the ground beneath her shook and gave way, letting her fall into an abyss of feeling.

Their lips fit together perfectly, as if they'd been kissing for years. Kian knew it would be more than just a simple kiss; it was knowing that she was going to be a part of him, from now until his time was done.

As he pulled away, he leaned his forehead against Adalyn's, and whispered, "Oh, ya leave me breathless."

Feeling sassy, Addy said, "That was my goal."

He was about to lean down, again, to kiss her, when there was a loud noise from downstairs.

Kian pulled away, and ran down the stairs, Adalyn followed, still cautious while going downstairs. When she met up with Kian, he was standing next to her parents, and they were all standing outside, on the porch. "What happened?" She asked.

But as soon as her eyes followed theirs, she saw what they were looking at.....on the side of her parents garage, the word "Bitch" was written in a bright, red spray paint.

"Oh my Lord," Evelyn said, pulling out her phone to call the police department.

Kian instinctively pulled Adalyn over to his side, tucking her against him.

Adalyn looked at her parents' faces, and started to cry. "Who would do this?" She asked, and before they can answer, offered her own answer, "Tommy!"

Doug looked at his daughter. "Do you think he'd really do something this petty?" His daughter didn't talk, only gave him a look that indicated she thought this is exactly what Tommy would do.

"Bastard!" Kian said, gaining looks from the three of them. "I won't be apologizin for da word," He offered, "but I'll apologize for usin da word in front of the ladies."

Not trying to make light of it, but Evelyn couldn't help but follow it up with, "Don't worry, my daughter has no issues using much-needed expletives."

For the first time, since seeing the graffiti, the four of them actually smiled.

The first officer arrived about ten minutes later. Within the hour, there was a second one there. All four of them answered the questions, but no one had any proof of who would've done this.

Officer Collins, who arrived first, told them he would question the neighbors to see if they'd noticed anything, before leaving. The second officer took pictures of the area, in case there was something that could help identify the culprit.

Once again, Doug and Kian were going to Home Depot to get paint. But this time, the atmosphere was tense.

"I'll show that tool a ting or two," Kian growled.

Doug nodded, "I know how you feel." He turned onto Hwy 35 South, going toward Alvin, and added, "And I believe that karma actually comes around and bites you in the ass!"

Kian had never seen Doug this riled. He certainly couldn't blame the man for it as he was just as angry. "Doug," He mumbled, "I think I should say somethin…."

Just then, a car snaked into the lane, narrowly missing the front bumper. "Ass!" Doug yelled, and slammed his hand on the steering wheel, shutting Kian up.

Later, that afternoon, the men painted the side of the garage, covering up the profanity. It took two coats, but they did a great job.

Evelyn asked Kian if he wanted to stay for dinner, and he declined. Seeing the look of disappointment on Adalyn's face, he reconsidered for a moment, then decided to just go home.

As he drove, he wondered if he'd ever get the chance to run into that ass, and what he'd do if he did. A sadistic smile crossed his face, then he remembered that his mother always told him that violence was the last option. In this case, she'd probably make an exception and tell him to beat the ass bloody.

Adalyn picked at her dinner, feeling like today had been a giant roller coaster. Finishing the painting, and especially Kian's kiss, were the highs, and seeing that word on her parents' garage, and watching Kian and her father cover it up, were the lows.

"You're not going to believe this," Evelyn said as she walked into the breakfast nook, handing her phone to Adalyn. "I didn't see it earlier," She said to her daughter.

Picking up the phone, she pushed the button to start the voicemail, and sneered when she heard Tommy's voice say, "Listen, Evelyn, I really need to see Adalyn, please have her call me."

Adalyn had to use all of her self-restraint to keep from throwing the phone straight out the window. "Why won't he leave us alone?" She asked her mother.

Doug had just listened to the voicemail, and said, "I'm calling the police and we're going to get a restraining order against him."

Since the next day was Saturday, Adalyn didn't have any therapy scheduled, and stayed in bed until almost eleven o'clock. She was awake, she just couldn't muster the energy to get out of bed.

Evelyn popped her head into her daughter's room, to check on her. "Are you okay?" She asked quietly.

Addy turned over, tucking the covers up under her chin, she smiled at her mom. "I'm okay, just exhausted."

Coming into the room, Evelyn sat on the edge of the bed, reaching over and absently rubbing her daughter's arm. "How did you sleep?" She asked.

"Good, actually," Adalyn answered. "I feel very safe here with you and Dad."

Liking her daughter's frankness, Evelyn responded, "Well, I'm glad to hear that."

Sighing, Addy said, "It's just that, I think all this crap with Tommy will drive Kian away."

Smiling down at her daughter, Evelyn responded, "Oh, I think it'll take a lot more than some stupid actions from a stupid person, to drive Kian away from you."

"Do you think so?" Adalyn asked her mom.

Now it was her turn to be frank, "Oh my, the room practically sizzles when you two are in it," she fanned herself, "I remember those days."

Adalyn asked, "Don't you feel that way about Dad anymore?"

Evelyn nodded, then explained, "Yes, I truly do, but then it's different. You get to a point where there's so much more than just the butterflies and racing heart." She folded Addy's hand into her own, "There's a comfort in just knowing he's there."

"I'm always there," Doug added as he came into the room. He'd been wondering where his wife ran off to, when he noticed Addy's door open, and heard them talking.

Smiling up at her husband, Evelyn added, "And I'm thankful for it, every day."

Throwing off her blankets, Adalyn growled, "Geez, you two are making me miss Kian, cut it out."

Doug laughed, "Okay, we'll leave so you can get dressed."

When Adalyn looked in the mirror now, she felt better. She'd really built up her muscles so now she looked healthy. She was naturally lean, but at least she didn't look as pale and ghostly as she did in the hospital.

When she came out of the bathroom, after brushing her teeth, and hair, she saw her parents in the kitchen, looking upset. "What's wrong?" She asked, feeling on edge immediately.

Without saying anything, Doug handed his daughter an envelope. There was a contract inside, from Adalyn's old agent. It was for an interview with her, her parents, and Tommy." The rage building up inside of her was too much, and without answering, she left the kitchen.

Her parents followed her, down the hall, and into the office on the front porch. Marching over, she turned on the shredder, then fed the contract into the machine. "And that," She said, looking up, "Is how you take care of trash."

She walked back out of the office, and toward the living room, Doug and Evelyn just standing there, watching her.

After a light lunch, Adalyn asked her father if he would take her out driving. They went to the local college since there was a giant parking lot there, without too many obstacles.

Doug was patient, knowing that her eagerness would make her a little jittery. He explained the basics, just like he did when she was fifteen, and just got her learner's permit.

They swapped places, and Adalyn got in, behind the wheel. She did all the required checks, and adjusted her seat so she could see. Putting the car into gear, she drove slowly, turning when her father told her to, and even parking properly.

"Just like riding a bike," Doug said, reassuringly.

Looking at her dad, Addy said, "Not unless a bike weighs a ton and could kill people."

There was more than sarcasm and humor in the statement, so Doug asked her to shut off the car. "Are you afraid?" He asked.

Adalyn nodded, "A little." She rested her forehead on the steering wheel for a second, then said, "I'm afraid that I'll black out, or forget, and hurt someone." She looked over at her father, "It's a miracle that no one else was hurt in my accident, you know that right?" She asked.

"I know," Doug answered. "Do you want to know about it?" He asked her in return. There was no reason to keep anything from her.

She'd heard about it from her mother, but not him. She stared out the windshield for a minute, then nodded to her father.

Leaning back, Doug turned, so he was facing her, and started, "Well, when we got the phone call, we were still in South Houston, so it took us a while to get up there to you."

Quiet, Adalyn just watched him.

"Your mother was beside herself, and I was barely hanging on," He wiped a tear from his eye, "I know that when you have kids you'll realize that there is a time when you can't take away all the hurt, and it's the worse feeling in the world."

Now Addy started to cry.

Doug blew out a breath, "We got to the hospital, and you were in ICU. There were all these machines, tubes, and God knows what they had you hooked up to." He clasped Addy's hand, "We went into the waiting room, about an hour later, and found Tommy and Jeni standing there. They looked like they'd just had a fight. Jeni was crying, and Tommy wouldn't really look at us."

She squeezed her dad's hand, to let him know it was okay to go on.

"Well, your mom knew something was up, and asked Jeni what happened. Jeni caved immediately, admitting that you'd walked in on her and Tommy and then went tearing out of his place, fast." Your mother sat there, very quiet, so I knew she was ready to explode. "Anyway," He sighed, "Tommy didn't even try to deny it, he just shrugged it off."

That didn't surprise Addy, and she just rolled her eyes.

Doug looked out the windshield now, "And then the doctors came in and said that they had the paperwork for us to sign, to you know, shut off the machines."

Addy's heart ached for her parents. They never should have gone through this.

"Your mother jumped up and literally knocked the clip board out of the nurse's hand, and screamed that she would never shut off the machines," He hated remembering the pain of that time, but he would endure it for his daughter's sake.

Smiling, Addy commented, "I'll bet she was pissed."

Doug's eyes widened, "Oh, pissed doesn't even begin to cover it. She screamed at the doctors, asking who said they were going to turn off the machines, and the nurse pointed at Tommy." He smiled, "I think she would've killed him, right then, had I not stepped in between them."

She didn't want her dad to have to relive this anymore, so Addy said, "Well, it would've solved some problems for sure if she would've killed him, but it's better that she's not in jail."

Chuckling at her attempt to help him, Doug gave her a hug. "Well, let's get home to Mama Bear before she takes out that nasty temper on us."

They switched places, and Doug started up the car to drive home.

Chapter 20

Sunday, Adalyn called Kian. Her parents took her out the day before, to get her a phone. She'd used her mother's enough to get the basic concept, and made Kian her first call.

Not recognizing the number, Kian wasn't sure he should answer, until he saw Alvin, TX on the caller ID. "Hello," He said.

"I got my very own phone," Addy said brightly. "And you're the first person I wanted to call."

Kian smiled, "Am I not the luckiest of men, then?" He asked her.

Now Adalyn beamed, and replied, "I think you are."

He laughed at her teasing, and asked her, "Would ya like to go out on a proper date tonight?"

Walking into her room, to give herself a little privacy, Addy asked him in return, "What constitutes a proper date?"

"I'm thinkin, dinner and a movie, how does that sound?" He propositioned her.

Nodding into the phone, and then laughing when she realized that Kian couldn't see her, she answered, "Oh, yes, that would be wonderful!"

Kian cleared his throat, trying to tamp down on his excitement, "Okay, I'll come and collect ya around five o'clock."

Adalyn returned, "Okay, I'll see you then." She disconnected the call, and then yelled, "Mom, can you help me?"

Evelyn came rushing into the room, and asked, "What's wrong?" in a rushed voice.

"I don't have anything to wear for my date with Kian tonight," Adalyn answered in a serious tone.

Trying to hold back her laughter, Evelyn nodded, trying to respect her daughter's difficulty. "No problem, we'll have Dad take us to the store and get you something."

Grabbing her purse, Addy said, "I'd like to pay for it myself," she was going to be insistent, if necessary, "It's important for me to start supporting myself."

Surprised, even though she probably shouldn't be, Evelyn agreed to Adalyn's request, and answered, "Sure, that's understandable."

Within the hour, the three of them were back at the shopping center, the girls went to before. It was easier this time, for Adalyn to handle the other people. She picked out a simple dress, done in a pale pink, with a gray trim. The design on it was little flowers, trimmed in the gray. It wasn't something Adalyn would've picked out before the accident, preferring some high end designer, because that was what was expected of a model. Now, she looked for comfort, as well as beauty.

"Perfect," Her mother commented, when Adalyn came out of the dressing room. "Now, shoes," She pointed back to the dressing room, to hurry her daughter along. They went over to the shoe department, and Addy panicked for a moment.

There were all these mile-high heels displayed, and she knew that she'd never be able to maneuver in them. She was lucky she kept her balance with flats on, these days. "What do we get?" She asked her mom, her voice laced with worry.

Evelyn rubbed Addy's arm, "It will be fine," she reassured her daughter, then steered her over to where the sandals and flats were. They picked out a few pairs together, and settled on a pair that matched the dress's pink color.

Doug was waiting outside, in the car. He'd run his own errands but was done in time to pick up his girls. "How did it go?" He asked them, as they got into the car.

"We got the perfect outfit," Addy answered, a smile on her face. "Mom," She said as they started toward home, "Will you help me with my hair and makeup?"

Evelyn looked at her husband, her own smile one of delight, "Sure."

As soon as they walked in the door, Adalyn raced off toward the bathroom, to shower.

Doug sat in the kitchen, with his wife, and asked, "So, a date, huh?"

Giving her husband a dry look, and commented, "Like you didn't see that coming a mile away…"

He sighed, and replied, "I don't have to like any man, when it comes to my daughter, but at least Kian respects her and treats her well."

Leaning over, Evelyn kissed her husband softly. She whispered, "He reminds me a little of you, years ago, and without that lovely Irish accent."

Now Doug smiled, "I love you," he said to her, and meant it every day.

"I love you too," Evelyn returned, and kissed him again.

Adalyn came out of the bathroom, and saw her parents kissing in the kitchen. The sight made her happy and envious at the same time. Her parents' marriage always seemed so solid. Without letting them know she was there, Adalyn left to go to her room to get dressed.

With her mother's help, Adalyn left her hair down, and only put a few curls in it to give it some body. Her makeup was light, but made her feel pretty. She came out into the living room, and did a little twirl, so her dad could see the whole outfit. "What do you think?" She asked him eagerly.

Doug stood up, and walked over to his daughter, smiling. "I think you are too pretty to be going out, and you should stay here with your mom and me."

Laughing at his teasing, Adalyn shook her head, and answered, "I'd love to; except I already promised Kian I would go." She pretended to pout, for his benefit.

Evelyn saw the lights turning into the driveway, and said, "Okay, he's here, why don't you go and get your bag," She said to Adalyn.

Giving her dad a peck on the cheek, Addy rushed down the hall to her room.

Kian knocked on the door, and was nervous. He shouldn't be, by now he'd been to Adalyn's house dozens of times. "Yes, but now you're taking her out," He said out loud, to himself.

Evelyn opened the door, a big smile on her face. "Kian," She said warmly, "come in."

As he came inside, he saw Mr. Phillips, and nodded to him.

Doug nodded back to Kian, and then reached out to shake his hand, saying, "You take care of her."

"She'll not be in any harm's way," Kian assured him.

When Adalyn came out of the room, she was nervous. She literally could not remember the last time she got dressed up for a date, and she wasn't sure she knew what to do. It was almost comical since she and Kian saw each other so much, and he knew her house as well as his own. She took a breath, and announced, "I'm ready."

Kian turned around. His stomach fell into his feet, and his breathing increased. "Oh, yer a dream, you are," He whispered.

His words made Addy's heart skip a beat. "Thank you," She said shyly, and walked over to take his outstretched hand.

Evelyn walked them to the door; waving as they got into the car and pulled out. When she saw the car leave, she turned back around to see her husband sitting on the sofa, sulking. "That's enough!" She said, and went over to him, plopping down on the sofa beside him, she said, "We're all alone."

Doug found something to smile about after all. "We are, aren't we?" He said, standing up, and taking his wife's hand to lead her down the hallway to their bedroom.

Kian didn't know where to take Adalyn. Normally, he would have asked his date in advance what type of food she liked. He and Adalyn had spoken for hours about everything, except the things that would help him on their date. "I'm feelin nervous," He admitted as he drove them toward Pearland.

"Thank God," Adalyn sighed, "I am too."

Her declaration eased his nerves. "I was thinkin that we shouldn't feelin this way, seein as we've spent so much time together, and we've already kissed, but I tell ya, it put me on edge, coming over to get ya."

Giggling, Adalyn looked over at him. "I was thinking almost the same exact thing."

"Well, that settles my heart a bit," He replied. "Where do ya want to eat?"

Addy had to take a few minutes to think about that. Where did she want to go? The thought popped into her head, and she blushed as she answered, "I'd like to go to your place, and we can order in."

Even though he was looking at the road, trying very hard to concentrate on getting them to their destination safely, he was having a tough time breathing and thinking. "Uh," He mumbled, "What do ya mean?" Luckily the street light turned red, so he could stop, and look at Adalyn.

When she looked over, into Kian's eyes, Adalyn wanted to melt. He knew her meaning, and she knew her meaning, but they both just needed to decide if this is where they were going. "I haven't felt like this in........maybe forever," Adalyn started, "I don't want to waste any time sitting in a crowded restaurant, making small talk, when we both want this."

Kian stared at her, swallowing hard. "Uh," He said again, "Okay," but his voice sounded different. The temperature in the vehicle jumped up a thousand degrees and he felt so "aware."

At the next light, Kian turned onto Broadway St. which was the main street that went through Pearland. They passed the strip malls, filled with small, but upscale shops, the thrift shops where you could find any antique you wanted, and the chain stores that filled up cities in an effort to make the American Dream a reality.

Neither of them spoke, both feeling the tension fill the confined space in his car.

To keep her mind occupied, Addy looked around the car. It was a newer, midsize sedan, and wasn't pretentious in the least. It was exactly what she expected Kian to have, a sense of practicality combined with the gadgets that men gravitated toward in their "toys."

"I like your car," She commented absently, trying to break the mountain of tautness that stood between them. It felt as if her insides were a rubber band, stretched to its limit.

Kian kept his eyes straight ahead, on the road, and answered, "Thank you," in a quiet, but intense voice.

Now the nerves swallowed her up again, and Adalyn worried that she'd pushed the boundaries. "Are you okay with this?" She asked him, her voice a little shaky.

They came to another red light, so Kian turned his attention from the road, to her. "I'll be honest, I wasn't expectin this, but I won't say I'm not thinkin all sorts of things."

"Like what?" She asked him, genuinely curious.

Now the conversation was turning into foreplay, as far as Kian was concerned, "I was thinkin how beautiful yer skin will look, like moonlight streamin through a window durin a full moon," he took her hand, bringing it up to kiss it. Instead of kissing the back of her hand, he turned their entwined hands, and kissed the tips of her, now upturned hand.

And Adalyn was lost, in the haze of want and need she desperately wanted to feel. His penchant for beautiful words was something that most men could never accomplish, and yet, Kian could have her imagining all sorts of things with just one sentence. She watched as his lips touched the tips of her fingers, and kissed them, one by one.

The light turned green so they had to move, which meant Kian needed to focus on the road. He didn't release her hand, only placed it on the counsel between them. He wouldn't break the physical connection between them until he absolutely had to.

Ten minutes later, they were pulling into his apartment complex, and Kian's nerves swelled up inside him again. He wasn't embarrassed about where he lived as it was a nice place, but he didn't own a home or have a sprawling home. He wondered what Adalyn would think of it. And he was silently praising himself for doing some cleaning before he left the house today.

Kian pulled into his designated parking spot, and shut off the car. He turned to Adalyn, and asked her, "Are ya sure you'd rather have somethin to eat here, and not go out?"

Looking at Kian, her eyes sparkling with awareness, Adalyn replied, "I think you'd better take me inside."

That was all the coaxing he needed. Kian released her hand, just long enough to get out of his side of the car, and come around to open her door for her. As he helped her out of the passenger side, he smiled, and pulled her to him for a kiss.

Their lips touched, and it was like spring exploding in a meadow that had felt winter's slumber for months, colors and scents spinning around in a whirl of growth. Their mouths meshed as if they were already lovers, from long ago, who knew the secrets each other carried.

When someone honked a horn, Adalyn jumped and stepped away. She was only slightly embarrassed about standing out in the open, kissing a man. "Sorry," She rushed the word.

Smiling, Kian reached out, and pulled her close once again, saying, "No need to be afraid, we'll be takin it as slow as you'd like."

Her spine stiffened, and she retorted, "I'm not afraid!"

"Of course you are, mo milis, because I am too," Kian whispered to her.

Chapter 21

They walked down the sidewalk, toward Kian's building. The sun was just beginning to sink low, casting long shadows across the lawns.

Adalyn looked around and saw that there were kids playing nearby, their laughter filling the air. People were coming and going, which was life when you lived in a complex. Suddenly, Adalyn was thrust back into a memory. It was of her own apartment, in Dallas. She was talking to a neighbor, and Tommy had just come up. He was rude to her neighbor, of course, and she remembered she had a niggling feeling that maybe she'd made a mistake.

When Adalyn stopped walking, and stared off, Kian began to worry. "Adalyn," He said softly, and was relieved when she looked over at him right away. "Were ya havin a spell?" He asked, worry tightening his gut.

"No," She answered, and squeezed his hand as they started walking again, "I was having a memory."

Intrigued, Kian asked her, "Was it a good one or bad one?"

Not trying to be difficult, Adalyn answered, "Neither, really. I think that I realized long before the accident that Tommy wasn't the one for me."

Just the mention of that idiot's name made Kian's blood boil. "Again, I'll be askin if that's good or bad?"

"Honestly," Adalyn replied, "I think it's very good." She started to swing their joined hands a little as they walked, "I think it tells me that I'm right where I'm supposed to be."

Truer words could not be spoken, as far as Kian was concerned. "I'll be thinkin so too, then." He winked at her.

And then, his neighbor, Missy came into their path. She halted for just a second, when she noticed Kian with Adalyn, and their joined hands. Kian felt a sting of worry trickle down his back. He thought his neighbor was a lovely woman, but he wasn't so blind that he didn't see that she had taken a shine to him. "Missy," He said with a smile as she neared them, "I'd like ya to meet Adalyn." He looked at Addy, and returned, "Adalyn, this is my dear neighbor, Missy."

Missy put her hand out to shake Adalyn's and was floored. The woman was gorgeous, with beautiful long hair, and a body that said "elegance." It was no wonder that Kian had fallen hard for her. "It's so nice to meet you," She said quietly.

"You too," Adalyn said.

The awkward pause that followed left them all fidgety. Kian spoke first, saying, "Well, we'll let you get on wit it then, it was good to see ya."

Nodding, Missy just smiled, and past them.

Adalyn waited about 30 seconds before commenting, "She's crazy about you."

Kian nodded, and said, "I suspected as much, but we've talked and she knew my heart was taken by another," he smiled when she shot him a look, and offered, "by you."

They came to a set of steps, and went up slowly. Although Adalyn appeared completely normal, she still struggled a little with some tasks. As they reached the top, she looked back at Kian, and said, "See, I'm getting better."

"And so ya are," He returned.

They walked down the hallway and reached the door to his apartment. He pulled out his keys, opened the door, and followed her inside.

Without waiting for Kian, Adalyn went exploring. She walked slowly around his spacious living room. Although he didn't seem too big on decorating, the furniture was nice, and looked comfortable. He had a book shelf that contained, what she assumed, were books related to his job since they had titles about muscles and therapy. There were also a couple of other books from authors she'd heard of. "Do you like to read?" She asked him, still perusing the titles.

Watching her, as she looked around his space, Kian felt exposed. He wanted her here, but wondered what she thought of his place. "I love to read," He said as he made his way to her.

She was still facing away from him when she spoke, "My mom keeps telling me I have to get back into practice, it will help me..." her words trailed off as she felt his hands on her shoulders. Turning slowly, she smiled. He was just inches away from her and his closeness made her pulse quicken.

"Are ya nervous?" He asked her.

Not able to answer, Addy just nodded yes.

Smiling, Kian pulled her close for a kiss. It was a quick one, but with plenty of punch, and left her reeling a bit when he released her to walk back over to the kitchen, saying, "You'll be havin your choice of Italian, Chinese, or Pizza," and he picked up the take out brochures.

Feeling as if she'd received a moment of reprieve from her nerves, she chuckled and enthusiastically said, "Chinese!"

Kian felt her relax, which helped him settle down. "That sounds good to me," He picked up the phone while he handed her the brochure.

They ordered the food, and Kian offered her a bottled water while they waited. He had wine in the refrigerator but he didn't want either of them under the influence of alcohol tonight.

Sitting down on the sofa, Adalyn waited for Kian to join her. "How long did they say?" She asked him.

"We've got a good twenty minutes, and they're pretty good at deliverin on time," He answered, then took a drink of his own water to wet his parched throat.

Adalyn scooted closer to him, "Twenty minutes huh?"

Kian saw the gleam in her eye, and laughed. "I don't think we can accomplish that much in a mere twenty minutes," He said jokingly, trying to play it off.

Moving closer still, Adalyn turned so she could snuggle into Kian's side. "That's fine, how about we just be close then?" She asked him.

He grabbed the remote with his right hand, as he wrapped his left arm around Adalyn, softly playing with a strand of her auburn hair. Turning on the television, they found a comedy to watch while they waited for their food.

Even with the distraction of the show, they both felt the tight string of need that connected them.

The doorbell rang a few minutes later, and Kian was relieved for the distraction. He wanted to kiss Adalyn so much, his body practically vibrated. Grabbing the bags, and giving the delivery guy a hefty tip, he turned around and took the bags into the dining area.

Adalyn joined him, grabbing the paper plates he put on the counter earlier, along with napkins and forks, and joined him.

"This isn't exactly what I had in mind, for impressin you on our first official date," Kian told her as they sat down, and scooped out rice and entrées onto their plates.

Looking at him, she asked, "What did you think I needed?"

Her words were interesting. Needed was not what he would have thought she would say. He assumed there would be words like expected or deserved, instead she trusted him. It humbled him and excited him at the same time.

"I'm not sure what you need, I only know that you deserve a beautiful dinner and to be waited on," He answered her questions.

Adalyn gave a very unladylike snort, "Well, you were wrong. I'm actually having a beautiful dinner," she took a bite of her food and smiled, "and I was waited on, so I'm set."

They continued to eat, talking about restaurants they both liked, and things Adalyn used to do for fun when she lived in Dallas.

Everything she said entranced him. Even with all she'd been through, she retained just enough of the childlike awe of discovery but didn't seem sheltered. She knew her own mind, and wasn't afraid to speak it.

Dabbing her lips with her napkin, Adalyn was full. She hadn't eaten much, the nerves kept nipping at her insides. "May I use your restroom?" She asked Kian.

"Yeah, it's just through the bedroom there," He pointed to the room, and flushed a little at the thought of her being there, in his private space.

As Adalyn got up, he stood to start cleaning up their dinner. It wasn't difficult since he just needed to toss out the plates, put the containers in the refrigerator, and wash up their utensils. When he was finished, he still hadn't seen Adalyn so he went down the hall to look for her.

He walked into the bedroom, expecting to see the bathroom door closed with her in there. Instead, he saw Adalyn, sitting on his bed, running her hands along the soft comforter. She'd slipped off her shoes and, as he looked at her, thought everything about her was so cute, and seductive. "Are ya alright?" He asked, his voice rough.

Looking up at him, Adalyn smiled, "Yes, I'm just waiting for you."

The words hung there, between them.

Kian took a step toward the bed, "Why were ya waitin for me?" He asked her.

Her eyes never left his, although she stretched out on the bed, "I was thinking that you would make love with me."

Again, those words floated around them, like clouds thick with moisture, waiting to pour down.

He stood next to the bed, and looked down at her, laying on his pillow, in his bed, and knew his life would be changed the moment he touched her.

Adalyn reached up, and pulled him down to her.

Trying to be gentle, Kian managed to move her over as he slid onto the bed. They were stretched out, front to front, and holding hands.

"Are ya sure?" Kian asked one more time. He didn't want to rush her in any way.

Adalyn cleared her throat. "Can you kiss me please?" She asked him.

There wasn't anything short of a bomb that would keep Kian from feeling her lips on his. He moved closer, and captured her lips with his.

The kiss enveloped them in warmth immediately, Adalyn opened herself up, wanting to get closer, and so she deepened the kiss. His tongue was soft, and skilled at twirling around hers, and making her feel as if she were lifted up into a level of physical awareness she'd never felt before. A moan escaped her as he began running his fingers up and down her arms, from her shoulders to her fingertips.

Adalyn twisted, so she was half over him, and his arms wrapped around her waist, holding her as if she were the only thing he needed to exist. "Kian," She spoke in between kisses, "this feels so good."

"Oh yes," Kian returned, still kissing her. He couldn't get enough of her taste.

Running her hands up his arms, and grasping onto his shoulders, Adalyn shifted again so now Kian was over her. It allowed her hands the freedom to make their way down to the bottom of his shirt, which was luckily, untucked, and get her hands underneath it. He was solid, not ripped like those guys on the cover of the magazines, but definitely had defined muscles. She felt his skin react to her, prickle as her fingertips moved across it. "You feel so good," She said.

Kian was unable to focus his mind on anything but the feel of Adalyn beneath him. He managed to pull up the hem of her dress, feeling her legs as they parted. He shifted so he was now hovering over her body, with her legs snaking around his. He began to trail kisses down her neck, nipping at her shoulder, and loving the taste of her.

It was strange somehow, to have Kian touch her with this kind of need and yet show her tenderness. He'd basically touched her whole body during their physical therapy sessions, and yet, there was never this kind of sensational emotional connection. "I love the way you feel," She whispered to him.

With her dress now pulled up, and him settled between her legs, he could feel the warmth of her, even separated by the fabric of his jeans. It made his body respond with more craziness, "I love the way ya taste," he nipped her shoulder, "I love the way ya feel," he stopped and raised himself up so he could look into her eyes. "I love you," He said, his face serious, and very still.

Adalyn looked up at him, poised above her, and knew the words he spoke were true. "I love you too," She answered, and pulled him back down to kiss her again.

This time, the kisses were rushed, vicious but sensual, they both started grabbing at clothes, groping for control, and reveling in the raw sexuality they both wanted to express.

Within a minute or two, clothes were discarded, and they were sitting, facing one another, with Adalyn cradled on Kian's lap. She could feel his hardness against her, and yet wanted to prolong that first moment when they joined their bodies. A thin sheen of sweat, probably from anticipation, covered her skin. She kissed Kian deeply, trying to feel every part of him.

Cupping Adalyn's bottom, Kian moved her forward so they were touching in the most intimate way. He wanted her, but also needed to protect her, so he stopped for a moment, and reached for the drawer in his nightstand.

Adalyn was taut with want. She didn't think she could last much longer without feeling Kian inside of her. With trembling hands, she helped him sheath his hardness, then guided him inside her slowly.

Every inch of his body screamed with need, and as he entered her, Kian felt a completeness he'd never known in his life. She was so tight, and wet and her face reflected the same excruciating need he knew was written on his. A moan escaped him when she began to move.

Adalyn couldn't play safe and didn't want to. Not about this….this was something she desired with every ounce of her body. He filled her physically, and emotionally. She moved over him, wrapping her legs around him, she let her head fall back, and smiled when he took advantage of her exposed neck by kissing it. "More," She breathed out.

He wouldn't deny her anything right now. He quickly turned them so he was now over her, placing her legs around his torso, he thrust into her with a ferocity he didn't even know he possessed. Caught up in his physical needs, he started speaking to her in Irish, "Is breá liom tú."

It didn't matter what he was saying, the words were beautiful and melted her body further into the tidal waves of need pulsing through her. She understood now what it felt like to be consumed, her need for Kian was unlike any yearning she could have imagined. She reached up and clung to his shoulders as the first surge of her orgasm came pushing through her body.

Kian watched her reach her climax, and knew it wouldn't take him long to follow, with another thrust, he felt himself tip over into the well of sensations.

They collapsed together, both breathing heavy, and snuggled on the bed, the evening light fading outside the window.

Chapter 22

Adalyn woke up, and found herself tucked in beside Kian in his bed. She must've fallen asleep, because they were covered with a blanket.

She moved slowly, trying not to wake Kian up, and made her way into the bathroom. After using the bathroom, and washing up a little, she made her way around the room, to find something to wear. She came across Kian's t-shirt so put that on. Padding out into the hallway, she noticed another door and, curiosity getting the better of her, she opened it.

It was his home office, if the desk and stacks of paperwork were any indication. His bag, the one he brought to their physical therapy sessions was sitting by the door, the table he used folded up and leaning against the wall.

As she made her way into the room, she saw another book shelf. Turning on the desk lamp, the room flooded with soft light.

She ran her fingers over the top of the desk, wondering what Kian thought about when he was working. She saw his pen and notepads there, along with a picture. Picking it up, she saw a much younger Kian standing there with another boy, and who she assumed were his parents. They looked happy, which made Addy smile.

Setting down the picture, her eyes caught sight of another table in the corner of the room, with papers scattered all over it.

The desk lamp didn't give her enough light so she flipped on the overhead light switch, and walked over to the table.

There were newspaper clippings, a large map, and magazines that Addy recognized as ones that she did shoots for. Picking up the first clipping, she read it, and her blood ran cold. It was the newspaper reporting of her accident. The picture of her mangled car brought a tear to her eye. She was so lucky that she was alive right now. Hearing a noise behind her, she turned to see Kian standing in the doorway. The look on his face was not a happy one and she felt like she'd done something wrong. Putting down the clipping, she offered, "I'm sorry, I was just snooping."

When Kian woke up, and Adalyn wasn't next to him, he got up immediately. Finding her in his office and looking at the newspaper article about her accident made his blood run cold. "Do ya know what that is?" He asked her, trying to remain calm.

"It's from my accident," She answered. But, then she looked down, and saw another clipping. "What's this?" She asked as she started to read it. The words took a bit to sink in, but she felt like something was off, and asked him, "Why didn't you tell me that your parents were in an accident the same day I was?"

Kian entered the room, feeling off kilter. He knew what he was about to tell her would hurt them both, but it was time to come clean. "I've been tryin to tell ya for some time now," He said in a shaky voice. "Remember when we went for the walk, and then when we were upstairs, I tried to tell ya....." his voice drifted off.

Her breathing shallow, from fear, Adalyn asked him, "What were you trying to tell me?"

He crossed the distance between them and guided her down to the chair. Grabbing his office chair, he rolled it over so he was sitting down, facing her. "Okay," He started, "I think it was so strange that your parents happened to have you transferred down here, to da facility that my company is contracted for." He took her hand in his, and noticed that she didn't hold his in return, "Anyway, I was talking to your mom about yer accident, and somethin struck me funny about it."

Adalyn didn't say anything, she couldn't. All she could give him was a quick nod, to urge him to continue.

"I remembered the day of my parents' accident." He began. "You see, my brudder, Kurtis, had a drinkin problem." The tears started coming down his cheeks. "I told my parents that he needed help, you see, and they wouldn't listen."

None of what he was saying was making sense to her, so she snapped at him with, "Kian, tell me!"

Taking a deep breath, Kian said, "I think my brudder caused your accident."

Even hearing the words, and knowing, somewhere inside, that he was going to say them, didn't prepare her for them. "Why do you think that?" She asked him, her body shaking.

He stood and helped her up. They turned to look at the map he had laid out. "Ya see here?" He asked, and waited for her to nod, "This is where yer accident happened." He pointed to another point, only a couple of inches away on the map. And, about thirty minutes after that, my brother crashed his car, and my parents were with him."

"So, why does that make you think he had something to do with what happened to me?" She asked him.

Pointing down at the map again, "Because his house is here," he said, "and he would've had to take this route to get to my parents' house."

Looking at him, she demanded, "So, why don't we just ask him and find out?"

Kian couldn't look at her, he answered, "Because he's dead." He waited to compose himself, and added, "He's dead and my parents, well, they were both hurt badly." He took a breath, "I trained to be a physical therapist so I could help em, but they both were just never the same, and died within a year of da accident."

So, he was saying that his brother may have contributed to not only the disintegration of his family, but her loss of three years with her family. Not saying anything, she went into his room, and started to get dressed.

Kian let her go, knowing she needed a little bit of privacy. When he did go into the bedroom, she was dressed, and grabbing her purse.

"I'll be takin ya home," He mumbled, and slipped on the t-shirt she'd discarded when she got her own clothes on. It smelled like her, sweet and exotic.

The drive back to her parents' house was as tense as the drive to his apartment, just for a very different reason. About halfway there, she asked him, "So why tell me?" She looked over, "Why not just leave it be? I would've never known."

Those questions were the very ones he'd been struggling with for over a year now, since he met her family. At first it was guilt, but helping her eased that. Now, he was afraid, afraid that the very truth he felt he needed to give her, was the one thing that would tear them apart. "Because, to love ya meant ya knowing all there was to know."

Usually his beautiful accent and colorful words made her feel better; now they just added to her frustration. "But if your brother caused my accident, how come the police didn't put two and two together?" She needed to know all of it now.

"My thinkin is… because the two accidents happened in different counties, with different first responders, and yer car ended up in a flooded ditch, there was no trace of any other car because of da damage and da water." He explained.

Now anger filled her, and she spat out, "So now you're a CSI?"

He couldn't hold his temper any longer, even with Adalyn, he had his limits. "Do ya think I wanted to tell ya this?" He yelled, his words reverberating around the car. "I knew what this would do, make ya angry, and possibly make me lose ya."

He pulled into the driveway at her parents' house, and she was opening the door before he even put the car in park. "Don't get out," She said in a tight voice, and got out, slamming the door behind her.

Kian watched as she went up the stairs and into the house. He saw the kitchen light turn on, and could see her mother in the window. Before he gave into his need for her, he put the car in reverse and backed out of the driveway.

Evelyn stood in her kitchen, listening to the story her daughter was giving, and was in shock. When Addy finished telling her the fantastical tale, she sat down, staring into space. Finally she asked, "Is he sure?"

Sitting down beside her mother, Adalyn answered, "He thinks so."

Looking at her daughter, Evelyn knew that she'd been intimate with Kian. A woman just knew these things, and now her daughter would need to make a lot of decisions. "What do you want to do?" She asked Adalyn.

So confused, Adalyn couldn't think straight. All of this information just blew her away and it was hard to discern her feelings about this with her feelings about Kian and their lovemaking. She felt like her feelings were a giant, tangled ball of yarn. She turned to her mom, and answered, "I think that I need to think."

Evelyn watched her daughter get up, and make her way down the hall toward her bedroom. Her heart broke thinking of what Addy had already gone through, and now what she might have to go through now.

The next morning, Adalyn woke up late. She imagined this day being a lot different when she made the choice to go to Kian's place yesterday. Now, she was lying in bed and staring up at the ceiling. She heard her parents get up earlier, and knew she should get up, but she was still confused.

Finally, she took a deep breath, and made her way into the kitchen. As soon as her father saw her, he stood up and wrapped her into his arms. Adalyn squeezed him hard, loving him more for being so protective. Her mother brought her a cup of coffee and sat down across from her at the breakfast table.

"Obviously, Mom told me about Kian's suspicions," Doug started. He took a moment to collect his own thoughts, before telling her, "I have to say two things to you, and then you can let us know what you want to do...." He said. "First," Doug grabbed her hand and squeezed it, "I don't care what happened three years ago because we have you back." At the outrageous look she gave him, he smiled, and continued, "If there was any way we could change something, then maybe I'd feel differently." He looked at his wife, "But Mom and I stayed strong, stayed together, and stayed with you." He waited for her to look up at him, and went on to say, "Second, if you and Kian really love one another, I think it's admirable that he wanted to open himself up to this kind of ridicule, not only from you, but from us."

Her father gave her a lot to think about. And, for some reason, his words made her feel like maybe there was a way for her to reconcile it all.

That afternoon, Adalyn called Kian's phone. Surprisingly, he didn't answer. She didn't think he would avoid her and looked at her watch. Given that it was early afternoon, she was pretty sure he was with one of his patients, and waited for the message to beep so she could leave a message. "Kian, it's Adalyn and I need some time," She took a breath, "I'll let you know when I've figured this out."

After hanging up, she went into the kitchen and told her dad she was ready to go to her counseling appointment with Christie, at the center.

Kian checked his phone after seeing his last patient, and was shocked to see he had a message from Adalyn. He waited until he was out into his car before listening to it. The words were like little knives, puncturing his heart over and over. She wanted time, and he couldn't deny her that. All of this, the falling in love, the making love, and the burden of thinking maybe his brother was responsible for all the pain her family suffered over the last three plus years, it was enough to make anyone feel overwhelmed.

When he disconnected the call, he wanted to find her and beg her forgiveness, but he knew that wasn't right either. If she needed space, she needed space.

Picking his phone back up, he dialed his boss' number and asked for a meeting.

Half an hour later, Kian was waiting to see his boss. Dr. Tillman had always been very invested in his job, and that was why Kian wanted to work with him. They were in this profession to help people, and Dr. Tillman understood that.

He opened his office door, and escorted a client to the door before motioning to Kian and saying, "Follow me."

They went into the office, and Dr. Tillman sat behind his desk. "So, what's going on?" He asked Kian.

Taking a deep breath, Kian started at the beginning.

When he finished the whole thing, including the fact that he and Adalyn had slept together, Kian waited for his boss to put him through the ringer about getting involved with a patient.

Dr. Tillman took in all of the information Kian gave him, and sat in his chair, astonished. When Kian finished the story, Dr. Tillman asked him, "So, are you going to keep treating her?"

The fact that his boss cut to the chase was part of what Kian respected about him. "I will if she'll allow it," He looked down at his hands, "But I'm thinkin she may not want it."

"Do you really think your brother had something to do with her accident?" He asked Kian. "It all seems so far-fetched."

That was something Kian couldn't deny.

Chapter 23

A month later, Adalyn sat in the office of a private detective in Houston. After her discussion with her father, she decided she needed to know for sure if what Kian suspected was possible and/or probable. Her dad made some inquiries and they met Mr. Wilkins. It turned out that this Mr. Wilkins had a mother who was also in the rehabilitation center that Adalyn stayed in. All of this "Six degrees of Separation" stuff was making Adalyn nervous.

Fortunately, Mr. Wilkins, as it turned out, was very good at his job. He contacted both law enforcement agencies that responded to the accidents. Looked at all the evidence, along with a forensics team he worked with.

All the "wanting to know" stuff was expensive, so Adalyn was once again, very thankful that she had some reserve funds in that account her parents hid from Tommy. It had been a month of waiting and wondering what really happened and she was exhausted, physically and emotionally.

She hadn't spoken to Kian since leaving him that voicemail. She went to a doctor's appointment the following week and he felt she didn't need the physical therapy or speech therapy any longer. Although she still saw Christie, to try to deal with the emotional ramifications of all of this, physically, she was as back to normal as she could be.

"Ms. Phillips," Mr. Wilkins said as he came into his office, "I'm so sorry to keep you waiting."

She wanted to be polite, and say it was fine, but it wasn't so she remained quiet.

He sat down, and pushed a file across his desk for her. He had a duplicate file in front of him, and opened it, so she did as well. "You'll see that we did a complete analysis of all the evidence at both scenes." He cleared his throat, "Personally, for Mr. Fitzpatrick to even make the connection, is nothing short of astounding. Neither agency seemed to have any clue, so it was a little tough getting them to cooperate at first."

Adalyn didn't bother to answer, or even look up. The file was very thick, and all this information was like looking in a book that was written in another language.

"But," He leaned back for a moment, looking a little smug, "we convinced them to do it, and it was interesting."

Feeling frustrated, Adalyn looked up and asked him, "What I want to know is, did Kian's brother cause my accident?"

Wilkins could appreciate her insistence. This was a different kind of case than he usually received. It took longer than he planned, but being a private investigator wasn't as rigid as being a part of law enforcement, so he could ask the questions that cops couldn't, or wouldn't. "It is the conclusion of both agencies, and my team, that although another vehicle certainly could have caused your car to veer off the road and into the ravine, there is no irrefutable proof that was the case."

Sighing, Adalyn retorted, "So you really don't know?"

Leaning forward, folding his hands together on his desk, "We don't know for sure, no, but we all think that the two accidents were coincidentally close in timeframe and distance, and that's where it ends."

Standing, Adalyn reached out to shake his hand, give him his final payment, and hightail it out of there.

"About that other matter……" Wilkins said before she could leave.

Sitting back down, Adalyn stared at him anxiously.

He leaned back and made a teepee with his fingertips, "We've discovered that the lady who did this was named Jennifer Parker."

At the mention of her ex-best friend, Jeni, Adalyn's eyes almost bugged out of her head. "What?" She asked him, shocked.

Shaking his head, Wilkins said, "We spoke to her, and she confessed, said she was pissed that her husband was so interested in you."

Poor Jeni, Addy thought, she'd never be in peace as long as she had Tommy in her life.

"Did you want me to contact Alvin Police Department so you can file charges?" He asked her.

Shaking her head, Adalyn replied, "No, it's done and no one was hurt."

Again, she stood, shook his hand, and, this time, she did leave the office.

She held the large envelope, with the file, close to her chest as she made her way down to the parking garage that adjoined the building.

Getting in the car by herself was still new. She'd gotten her driver's license only the week before, Dr. Cooper actually signed off of her request early so her dad and she practiced a lot. It was important to both of them that she should have this little bit of independence.

Pulling out of the parking garage, Adalyn glanced down at the report and wondered why she really wanted to know if Kian's suspicions were right. Her dad was right when he asked her if it really made a difference. She didn't feel like the information resolved anything inside of her. Kian's brother and parents were still gone, and she had still lost three long years in a coma.

And yet, here she was, alive, well, and driving her new car down the freeway to go home.

At the exit she knew her father took to get her to the rehabilitation center, she pulled off. It was a long shot for sure, but maybe she would get lucky. After all, she woke up from a coma after three years....how many people could say that?

First, Adalyn found a liquor store. After finding what she needed she got back into her car, and called her parents. When that was done, she took off to find Kian.

Pulling into the rehab center parking lot, Adalyn looked around for Kian's car. She smiled when she saw it, and went inside. The receptionist recognized her immediately and was about to say something when Adalyn put her finger up to her own lips as a signal to keep quiet. She asked the receptionist, "How would you like to help me out?"

Dr. Cooper was coming around the corner, and looked confused when he saw Adalyn Phillips standing there. He asked her, "To what do we owe the honor?" smiling at his own humor.

Adalyn smiled in return, and asked, him, "How would you like to be part of a conspiracy?"

"Sounds interesting," He answered, and followed her down the hall to his office.

Kian was working with Mrs. Wilkins and she was testing the limits of his patience today. Everything was about her son, and her grandkids, and about a three year old's birthday party and he wanted her to just focus on the exercises he was guiding her through.

He really needed to snap out of this pure rotten mood he found himself in. It wasn't Mrs. Wilkins' fault that he pushed away the only woman he loved, and now here he was, acting the gowl and not respecting his patient's time.

"Why don't you just call her?" Mrs. Wilkins asked Kian.

Surprised that she would know what his problem was, Kian replied, "Because I've been the gimp, Mrs. Wilkins, and it isn't somethin all women are forgivin for."

Mrs. Wilkins smiled, and patted his cheek, "For someone who has such a brave history and culture, you're kind of acting like a coward."

Her words set him on edge alright, he would defend himself, even to this old woman, if he had to.

She sighed, "I'm just saying, if you love someone, you just need to keep showing them until they forgive you."

Her words, although not an apology, were sincere and he appreciated them. "Thanks," He said and reached over to give her a peck on the cheek, "I'll be takin that into consideration."

As he packed up his bags, a few minutes later, Kian saw Dr. Cooper come into the room. He smiled at the doctor, and said goodbye to Mrs. Wilkins. She'd since moved on to regaling her roommate about the three-year-old's birthday party.

"What can I do for ya today, Dr. Cooper?" Kian asked as he zipped up his bag and tossed it over his shoulder.

Dr. Cooper smiled, "Well, I've got a new patient I'd like you to see," he said. "I've talked to Dr. Tillman and he thought you could fit in one more today."

Sighing, Kian nodded. If Dr. Tillman said he could, then he could. "Sure," He said to Dr. Cooper, "lead the way."

As they walked down the hallway, they talked about Mrs. Wilkins' progress, and about a few more patients. It seemed strange to Kian that they were walking down to the South Wing since that's where the worst off patients were. Immediately, his thoughts wandered to Adalyn. He wondered where she was now, and sighed when he thought of how miraculous she proved herself to be.

A minute later, they were walking into Adalyn's old room, and Kian felt self-conscious. He really didn't want to see a patient in this room, it made him think of her. He was about to say so to Dr. Cooper, when he saw Adalyn sitting there on the bed.

Shock filled his mind, then worry. He dropped his bags, and rushed over to kneel down in front of her. Inspecting her for signs of trauma, Kian asked, "What's happened?"

Adalyn stared at him as Dr. Cooper quietly left the room, closing the door behind him. She finally said, "It's more like, what didn't happen?" She answered him with a question.

Confused, Kian just stared at her. She was the most exquisite woman he'd ever seen. Her hair flowed over her shoulders in soft waves of rich auburn and he ached to run his fingers through it. "I don't understand."

Looking directly at him, Adalyn responded, "Well let me enlighten you.......first," she held up one finger, "I'm perfectly fine, so don't worry." He relaxed and she held up two fingers, "Second, I had someone look into the accidents, professionals," she saw that he wanted to interjected but she put her fingers on his lips to keep him quiet, "and all of them, from two different police departments and an independent team think that there was just a freaky coincidence between them."

Kian let the tears flow down his cheeks. Some men felt that crying was a sign of weakness, whereas he felt it showed that he felt.....and felt deeply. Knowing that his brother didn't share in the responsibility of her accident gave him an enormous sense of relief.

"Third," Adalyn held up three fingers, "I don't honestly think I would care if the outcome was different." She cupped Kian's face in her palms, and whispered, "Because no matter what kind of weird fate brought us together, it was the best thing to happen to me."

Nodding at her, Kian simply said, "And me too, mo milis."

Getting a little off topic, she smirked, and told him, "I looked that up you know."

Trying not to laugh, Kian asked, "You did?"

"Yes," She said, "it means my sweet."

Nodding, Kian answered, "Yes it does."

Growing serious, Adalyn asked him, "Do you still think I'm sweet, Kian?"

Grabbing her hands and bringing them to his mouth so he could kiss them, Kian replied, "I think ya're the other half of my body and soul and I pray to the saints daily that you'll forgive me."

"For what?" Adalyn asked him, shocked. "For being brave enough to be honest, even if it meant that we wouldn't be together?" She started crying, "If anything, that made you possibly the noblest man on the face of the earth."

Kian smiled, and asked her, "So what do we do now?"

Adalyn reached behind her, and brought around a brown paper bag. She reached inside and pulled out a bottle of very good Irish whiskey. "I think you said once that your father said something about nothing being better than the love of a good woman and good whiskey."

"I believe I did say somethin to that effect, yes," He answered.

Clearing her throat, Adalyn said, "Well, here's the whiskey, and I'm assured it's the best, and I've been told I'm a pretty good woman, soooooo how about you marry me and we'll just live the best life we can."

In his whole life, Kian couldn't imagine a better proposal.

He pretended to consider her offer, and smiled wide, saying, "I think I could handle the likes of you alright. But I'll tell ya, I've got a wicked Irish temper and a burnin for ya that may never go out."

Smiling at him, Adalyn leaned forward and gave him a kiss. When she pulled back, she said, "I think I can handle that."

An hour later, they were in Dr. Cooper's office, with her parents, and having a shot of the Irish whiskey and making plans for their future. And there was nothing so good, to Kian's way of thinking.

www.ingramcontent.com/pod-product-compliance
Lightning Source LLC
Chambersburg PA
CBHW050506260626
47157CB00004B/1215